Scarves & Sombreros

Neil Montagnana-Wallace with Mark Schwarzer

Foreword by Pelé

bounce books

www.bouncebooks.com

Copyright © Neil Montagnana-Wallace 2008
First published in Australia in 2008 by Bounce Books Pty Ltd.

National Library of Australia
Cataloguing-in-Publication data:

Montagnana-Wallace, Neil.
    Megs, Scarves and Sombreros

    Neil Montagnana-Wallace, Mark Schwarzer.

    1st ed.

    Rosanna, Vic. : Bounce Books, 2008.
    For children.
    ISBN 978090316728 (pbk.)

    1. Soccer - Australia - Juvenile fiction.
    2. Immigrant children - Australia - Juvenile fiction.
    I. Schwarzer, Mark. II. Title.

A823.4

Cover illustration by Daniel Tonkin, Iron Monkey Studios
(www.ironmonkeystudios.com)

Cover & Internal design by Bounce Books
(www.bouncebooks.com)

Photography by Enzo Liuzzi from Dog House Digital Imaging
(www.doghousedi.com) and from the family collection.

Edited by Gwenda Smyth

Distributed in Australia by Macmillan Distribution (www.macmillan.com.au)

Printed and bound by Tien Wah Press (PTE) Limited

www.megsmorrison.com

This one's for each and every one of the coaches whom I've had throughout my career, especially those I had as a young boy. If it weren't for their passion, dedication and love of football, I might never have fulfilled my potential.

Mark

This book is for the kids.

For any kids and all kids, but especially for my kids (and that includes you, Kid).

Neil

The Authors' Shout-outs

We'd like to say loud and clear how much we appreciate the work of the entire Megs crew – and not just the gang at Bounce Books. This has been another great team effort.

To everyone who has believed in the journey of Megs, thank you for keeping us going. And for everyone else who is getting on board, a big welcome: Pelé, Shep Messing, Afifa Saad, Football Australia, QANTAS, NAB, the Erdi Group of hotels, Linthorpe, Austrade, Javelin, International Quarterback and Iron Monkey Studios, not to mention those who have already enjoyed *Megs and the Vootball Kids*. Enzo and Dixy, you two are legends.

To the masses of football fans out there across the planet, this is your game. Thank you for making it so.

And finally, thanks to all the educators out there. Take a bow.

Foreword

"Mark Schwarzer met me when he was playing for Australia at the under 16 World Cup in Scotland. We took a picture then, but I didn't really know him. I am proud to say that I know him now. He has become a great goalkeeper for many years in the England Premiership and internationally for Australia. Much more important to me is that he is a great example for children. He has helped write a series of children's books that I think are important. Megs is a great example of how football speaks the same language to people all over the world regardless of their background, colour or religion. These books show how beautiful our game is – not just on the field, but for children growing up. Thank you, Mark, for what you have done for the children of the world."

Good luck,

Edson Arantes do Nascimento
(More famously known as Pelé)

ABOUT PELÉ

Athlete of the Century,
International Olympic Committee

Joint Player of the Century,
FIFA (shared with Maradona)

The only player to have three World Cup winner's medals

1280 goals from 1363 games in all competitions

92 Brazilian National Team appearances (77 goals)

Pele looking up to a young Mark Schwarzer in Scotland

Contents

Some Stuff You Should Know

FIXTURE – PENNENDALE WANDERERS		
Rounds 1 + 10	Vs	Bayside Blues
Rounds 2 + 11	Vs	Roverdale
Rounds 3 + 12	Vs	Hills Rockets
Rounds 4 + 13	Vs	Thornbury
Rounds 5 + 14	Vs	Penders Grove
Rounds 6 + 15	Vs	Trengal Tigers
Rounds 7 + 16	Vs	Brenthill Catholic
Rounds 8 + 17	Vs	Fairfield
Rounds 9 + 18	Vs	Southside Sharks

Team Line-Up *Game 1*

COACH	SUBSTITUTES	REPORTER
Atti Czibar	12. Adam	Val
	13. Mitch	
	14. Sam	

One | Not Quite a Hero's Welcome

'Whoa! What have we here? Did you wet the bed or something?' Mr Morrison laughed through half-eaten toast.

'Very funny, Dad. Is this what you're normally like at this time of day?' Megs replied cheerfully. It was the first time he had been up before his alarm (and some serious prodding from his parents) in the three months he'd been in Australia. And the fact that it was a school day – a Monday school day at that – made the occasion even more unusual. So his dad couldn't be blamed for teasing him.

'You know it's Monday, don't you?' his mum grinned. 'And you know school doesn't start for another hour? Still, it's good for you to realise the sun actually rises – and doesn't just appear the moment you happen to open your precious eyes.'

'Paloma'll be round soon, and we're going to catch up before school. I thought you'd be happy I'm up early – so don't tempt me to go back to bed.'

Things had certainly moved on since Edward 'Megs'

Morrison had arrived in Australia from the north of England what sometimes seemed like a lifetime ago, but at other times seemed like yesterday. He'd become friends with a wrinkly old school cleaner who'd turned out to be an ex-international footballer. He'd made new pals (or 'mates' as they were called here) who loved football as much as he did – almost – and he'd even managed to help form a new school team. And to top it off, in their first game last Friday, half the school had been there to see them demolish the Baystone Blues 5-0. So after initially dreading every step towards his new school, Megs was finding the world a much happier place.

'You got the papers, Dad?' Megs asked.

Mr Morrison slid the *Daily Telegraph* across the red-topped kitchen table, then pushed over the *Pennendale Press* as well. Megs wanted to look for the match report Val had written on their first game. She'd emailed it to all of them over the weekend, but even though he'd read it already, he was keen to see his name in print. There was something special about seeing your name in print.

But Megs was disappointed. The *Telegraph* only had a couple of paragraphs about world football that Megs already knew in much more detail after looking at the internet last night. And their result wasn't even in the summary listing of all the games across the state. In fact, none of the local results were there.

The *Pennendale Press* was equally unsatisfactory, even

though this time at least the game was mentioned. A careful search found a little article next to the lawn bowls results and above an ad for 'Barb and Pete's Bloomin' Great Nursery'. Not quite the bigtime, it had to be said.

PENNENDALE PRIMARY SOCCER – FIRST GAME, FIRST WIN

Pennendale Wanderers Primary School Soccer Team won 5–0 on Friday in front of a big crowd of people excited to watch the team's very first game in this year's Western Region Schools' Competition. In fact, it was the first game back after a long absence for the school, and after this result, the message to the other teams is – look out!

Nothing about the brilliant atmosphere, or about how more than half of the school were there cheering and clapping like crazy. Nothing about the Wanderers' complete domination of the match – and nothing about the nutmegs, the step-overs and the pace that had led to Megs's three goals.

But Megs was feeling so chirpy that he didn't let it get him down. Whether or not the papers said it, he knew he'd bagged a hat-trick from midfield, and he was secretly looking forward to everyone at school talking about it. And he was sure Paloma'd be positively bouncing this morning after she'd scored one goal and set up another for Jed 'the Simpfenator' in a great performance. Paloma walked with a spring in her step even on her worst day!

'Anything there?' Mrs Morrison asked, before taking the final sip of her morning cup of milky tea. She knew what her son was looking for, and loved the fact that he'd been so happy ever since the Baystone match. In fact, he'd been bright-eyed ever since they'd started official training with their new coach.

'Not really,' Megs replied. 'And they called us a "soccer" team and all. Val'll be pretty mad after the amount of effort she put into her report only to have it not used.'

'Well, if the team keeps playing like that, I'm sure the papers will take more notice,' Mrs Morrison consoled him. 'Now try and put your cereal in your mouth instead of all over your chin. And make sure you put your dirty dishes away. I've got some homework to do today, and I don't fancy cleaning up after you as well.'

Megs was pleased his mum was enjoying her computer course so much, but was much less happy about the extra stuff he was having to do around the house as a result. It was also weird to have a mum doing homework, and annoying to find himself feeling guilty if he wasn't doing as much as she was.

Before long, a knock sounded on the door, so Megs dropped his spoon, picked up his bag, and bounded down the corridor – calling out his goodbyes as he went. He was looking forward to seeing Paloma.

'Put your plate away!' Mrs Morrison called out from the study.

It was spooky how Megs's mum always knew what he was doing even though she was in another room. So

Megs quickly scurried back to the kitchen, put his plate in the dishwasher, then began his journey to the door anew.

'Teeth!'

Man, she was good.

'Just a minute,' Megs called out to the front door as a couple more knocks sounded. He hurried to the bathroom and gave his teeth a cursory brush that was as fast as Thierry Henry running down the wing for France, then finally made his way to the front door.

'Right, this time I'm off. See y' later,' he called as he reached for the door handle.

But it wasn't Paloma.

It was Vincent Braithewaite, his dad's boss and the Wanderers' team sponsor, standing on the front steps. And although his shoes were still as shiny as his slick black hair, he was without his customary suit and tie.

'Morning, superstar. How you feeling today?' Vincent ran a hand through his hair; his wide grin looked somehow forced. Megs was taken aback seeing him and not Paloma, but managed a smile.

'Pretty good, thanks,' he replied.

'Your dad in?' Normally relaxed and chatty, Mr Braithwaite was being unusually direct.

'Sure. He's reading the papers. Da-ad!' Megs called out as he saw Paloma approaching up Valetta Avenue.

Mr Morrison must've heard the conversation because he came to the front door wearing trousers and buttoning up a shirt, rather than appearing in the jocks and singlet he'd been sitting around in just moments before.

'Vincent! This is a surprise.' He sounded confused. 'Have you come to give me a lift to work? I haven't missed an appointment or something, have I?'

Megs saw his opportunity, hitched his blue backpack onto his shoulders, and hurried off between the two men towards Paloma.

'Have a good day!' Mr Morrison called after him as he and Mr Braithwaite went inside.

Megs was still a bit puzzled, and he had the distinct impression his dad was feeling the same. Mr Braithwaite had seemed uneasy, too.

'Hey, Megs.' Paloma greeted Megs with her trademark smile. 'Was that Mr Braithwaite? Did he come to congratulate you again?'

'Dunno. He came to see Dad, but he seemed a bit weird.'

Megs shrugged. There were more important things to talk about than early morning visitors. 'So... did you see the papers? Nothing besides a few lines in the local one,' he began.

'Doesn't surprise me,' replied Paloma. 'Until the Socceroos did so well at the World Cup, we were lucky to get anything on soccer in the papers. Things are getting better now, and the A-League gets pretty good coverage. Did your games make it into the papers in England?'

'Yeah, especially the local paper. Almost all the games get a report. If a team won 5–0 in their first-ever game, they definitely would. How did Val take it?'

'She's cool. Don't think she expected anything either,' said Paloma. 'But we all read the report on email, so she didn't waste her time. I think she's going to keep all the reports this year. It's funny how much she's into it now… she's never been interested in any sport before,' she added.

'Well, she played a big part in persuading Atti to coach. And it's good having her around the games and training. Reckon she'd ever join in?' asked Megs.

'Doubt it. She gets really nervous even thinking about team sports.'

'Really? Huh.' Megs found it interesting to discover that some people didn't like sport. He could kind of understand that some people didn't like football as much as he did, but being scared about sport in general? Who would've thought.

The pair walked through the front gates a good half -an-hour before school started, and Megs was shocked to see at least thirty-five kids in the schoolgrounds chatting, playing and enjoying the crisp, clear morning. Even with his good friends in England, he only ever got to school a minute before the bell went. It really was a different world Down Under.

'Hi, guys!' Paloma said a general hello to the group just inside the school gates. Of them all, only Lin and Paloma were in Megs's class and Megs was the only boy. Not one of them was a Vootball Kid. Before too long, Megs felt his excitement and pride starting to sag. Six girls and Megs. And no football chat. None of the hero's welcome that Megs had imagined, and he pretty soon wished he'd stayed in bed.

He looked around the schoolgrounds for anyone else who might be interested in talking about the game, but without luck. So the conversation raged all around him without his input. Television shows; how even though Justin Timberlake is hotter than Johnny Depp, Johnny is still definitely hot even though he's old; and then on to how younger brothers shouldn't be allowed to exist. Nothing Megs knew anything about, and as far as he was concerned, nothing that actually mattered.

Before long, Val walked towards the group. Her schoolbag was so big on her back she looked like an upright turtle. Her uniform was Monday-morning-crisp, topped off with her now-standard Pennendale Wanderers tracksuit top. She marched up to the group at a pace more compatible with Paloma's energy levels. It was clear something was on her mind.

'I've got some news.'

Two | Are. You. Kidding. Me?

'You sure?'

'Really?'

'Who gets to go?'

'How cool is that? Reckon you've got a chance?'

The girls were falling over themselves to get a word in, once Val had told them what she'd heard. Megs and Paloma were the only Vootball Kids among them and therefore the only ones for whom the news really meant anything, but they were also the silent ones. The news was taking time to process.

As the enormity of the news sank in, Megs finally spoke up.

'So hang on,' he said slowly, his eyes as wide as saucers, 'what you're saying is that the winner of this year's competition will go to England, including to Liverpool, to play over there. For a full three weeks. Are. You. Kidding. Me?'

'Well, that's what I heard.' Val could not keep the excitement out of her voice.

'Tell me again who you heard this from.' Megs was

trying to find a loophole in this amazing news. Surely it was too good to be true.

'Well, Mum is friends with someone who is on the Board of the Western Region of Schools. She was over last night, and I heard them talking about it. I don't know if it's supposed to be confidential, but they were pretty loud. I guess, because I don't like sport, they figured my overhearing wouldn't matter. So I didn't say anything, and just kept listening.'

'And it's at the end of this season?' Paloma asked, bouncing up and down on tippy-toes.

'Apparently so.'

'Well, why don't we know yet?' Megs the Doubtful continued suspiciously.

Then it was Lin's turn. 'Does it matter? Maybe you'll know soon. Imagine that – you get to go back to England! How cool!' She and Megs were now on quite good speaking terms after her initial snootiness when he had first arrived.

'Yeah, I know. That's why I want to be sure. It's too cool to not happen now that it's in my head!' Megs's stomach was churning. He certainly didn't want to go back to bed now!

'So how do you join the team?' asked a tall, blonde girl with ruler-straight hair that went all the way down to her bum. She wasn't in Megs's class, and he didn't know her well enough to tell if she was joking or not, but she wasn't smiling. Some of the other girls seemed to like the way she was thinking.

'Yeah, how many people are on a team? Surely you

can fit a few more in?' This whacked-out suggestion came from another tall girl (was everyone in this country bigger than Megs?) who only moments before had been leading the charge on the 'Johnny Depp is still hot no matter how old he is' argument.

At that point, Abda approached the group, limping slightly from a twisted ankle she'd sustained in the game against Baystone. Her fluttering headscarf made her look like she was moving even after she'd stopped.

'Abda, Abda! You'll never guess what Val's found out!' Paloma had to raise her voice to be heard.

'No, you're probably right,' replied Abda, smiling. 'With the stuff Val finds out, you'd have to be a magician to try and guess.'

'Ha ha,' Val commented good-naturedly.

'Well, it seems that whoever wins the Championship this year will be going to England to play some games and watch some EPL matches.' Paloma cut straight to the point. She was good at that.

'You're kidding!' But Abda could see she wasn't. This was for real. 'Is it for the top team at the end of the season, or do we have finals? The winner of the Grand Final, or winner of the Premiership?'

'What do you mean, finals?' Megs was a bit confused. Surely whoever had the most points at the end of the season was the champion. League competition wasn't a knock-out competition like the FA Cup – why have finals?

'There aren't any finals,' Val answered Abda. 'Whoever wins the League are champions and will get to go.'

'When do you train?' asked the girl with the hair that looked longer than Megs was tall.

'Mondays and Wednesdays straight after school,' answered Paloma. 'Come along if you want. The more the merrier!'

Megs's brow furrowed. How could she just give a general invitation to join the team? They couldn't allow any old people to wander in and out of the team as they wanted simply because there was a big prize to be won. Things had just got far too serious for that!

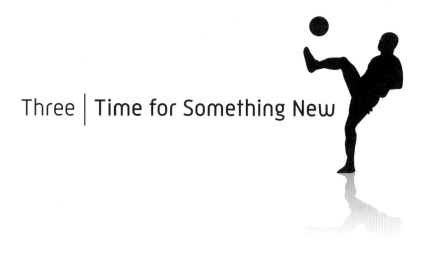

Three | Time for Something New

'Hello, you lot. Come over here so I see all you. I want see all of you.'

It was the first training session since the Wanderers' victory in Game 1 of the Western Region Schools Competition, and Atti was keen to get things underway. Although a relaxed, calm type of coach, he was taking to his new role like a fish to water and was serious about doing a good job. His eyes sparkled just that little bit more when he had his whistle around his neck and a bag of balls by his side.

'Now, you did good on the weekend. Very good. But it only game one of many games. All it was is a good start, and now we must prove we can do it again. And again. I happy, but we still not play enough as team. Sometimes we do, yes, but team is best thing and we must do it all the time. Team is what wins big games, and that is what we train on today.'

Atti's logic couldn't be argued with, but there was a murmur among the players nonetheless. By now every Vootball Kid had heard of 'The Trip' and was itching to know if it was actually true – not that Val had ever been wrong before! Why hadn't Atti said anything? Matteo caught Megs's eye as Atti spoke, and shrugged as if to say, 'Well, maybe it's not true.' Matteo was good at shrugging – it was as if his shoulders could speak.

Atti continued, 'Now, we have new players. Well, we have new people here to train who want to be players.' He welcomed Be as he gestured towards the tall blonde girl, then turned to the other tall girl.

'Actually I'm Catherine,' explained the blonde, 'and she's Be.'

Atti screwed up his face as he played along with everyone's laughter. 'Are you sure?'

Megs looked over at the two tall girls, and noticed that despite all the laughter they seemed decidedly more nervous now than when they had all been talking before school that day.

'OK – we warm up. Simpenate, you take them for jog around this dust bowl, and remember all the sideways, knees up, heels to bum, up for headers. Do good warm-up. Important.'

Megs couldn't really think of a time when it had rained since he'd arrived in Australia, and while it was something he'd boasted about to his friends back home, he was starting to see that it was actually a bit of a worry. The schoolgrounds were really just dust and weeds and had become increasingly dry and bumpy even in the time since Megs's arrival. The ball bounced around like a mini explosion every time it hit the ground, and this made it difficult to play. In fact, sometimes it made you look a fool. Luckily their pitch for matches was pretty good, but who would've thought that too much sunshine could be a bad thing? Certainly not the lads back in Liverpool...

The chattering began the second they started their warm-up. Everyone had been waiting for Atti to tell them that the Trip was for real. But he hadn't uttered a peep. Concern quickly spread, and however hard the Simpfenator tried to lead a good warm-up, it just wasn't working. By the time they got back around to Atti, the group was spread out, talking, and doing their own thing. Some had stopped warming-up altogether and were strolling back more interested in their conversations than in training. In short, they looked a mess.

'What kind of team is this? Some walk, some skip, some jog and all talk. You win one game and you think you already booked trip to England? That what you think?' There was a real edge to Atti's voice.

Silence – apart from the ticking of brains.

Slowly Atti's face creased like a scrunched-up piece of paper, before a flicker of a smile ran across his lips.

More silence.

Atti's little smile rapidly grew to Grand Canyon width. He was enjoying his team's discomfort.

Megs couldn't handle it any longer. 'Is it true, Atti? Tell us it's true,' he blurted out.

'Pardon?' Atti asked, feigning deafness, but really just milking the moment.

'This trip. You just mentioned going to England. Is it true or not?'

'Well, little Megs, it only true if you win the League. But yes... it definitely true.'

The pressure valve was released. The Vootball Kids exploded with claps, cheers and slaps on each others' backs. To England! To football in England!

Amid the excitement, Atti caught Megs's eye and shot him a happy little wink. He understood the extra significance of this news for his star player.

'But,' he then called out above the din, 'you not win nothing unless you train and unless you work as team. Now, let's forget that first load-of-rubbish warm-up and start again. Simpenate – off you go again. Now let's see what you can do.'

This time the warm-up was precise, professional and befitting a team who had eyes on winning a Championship.

Atti then put them through their paces with some sprint and agility work – all in little teams, and all with push-ups, sit-ups, or star jumps for the team which came last in each exercise. Next, he had the mini teams race each other through an obstacle course of cones while holding hands. To break the hold meant the race was lost, so everyone had to work together. At first, they were all a little bit worse than hopeless, but they gradually got the hang of it. When it became easy, Atti got the balls out and introduced something else.

Standing in a large square, seven players had a ball in their hands, and seven did not. Each player with a ball had to serve the ball to a player without, who was to volley it back to the server. After each turn, the players

16

would then randomly move on to another server who would do the same thing. Simple.

The trouble was, every time a player made a mistake and a ball hit the ground, all fourteen players had to go down and do five push-ups. It didn't matter who it was or when it happened, everybody paid the price. Even Atti got down and did his bit with his players. In five minutes, they'd all done 105 push-ups (Atti had to give up at sixty-five), and the coach's point was made loud and clear. It's a team, and everyone fails or succeeds together. A team wins together, and a team loses together.

'What else this teach you?' Atti asked.

'That 105 push-ups is a lot of push-ups,' said Max, looking rather like a gorilla with his tired arms hanging limp at his sides.

'True, but what else?'

'It's annoying doing push-ups when it isn't your fault. And you feel bad when it is,' suggested Abda.

'Good point. Be aware of team. Anything else?'

Silence.

'Well, is the skill easy? Here, Matteo, volley this back!' Atti served the ball, and Matteo prodded it back.

'The skill is easy and you can all do it. So why not do it right every time? Because you not concentrate, that's why. You think skill is easy, so you take it easy too – then you all do 105 push-ups which is not so easy. Point is, you must concentrate, and you must do the simple things right. Then you win games, and then you go to England. Let's do again – but this time the servers and volleyers change.'

After the next five minutes they had only totalled forty-five push-ups. Which was good, because the servers were struggling to hold their arms up just to throw the ball to the volleyers! Atti's point was crystal-clear.

'Good. Now, we play game. Six versus six with two goalkeepers. But thing is, each team must have three groups of pairs and they must hold hands always. No hold hands in the pairs – free kick to other team. Understand?'

With slippery, sweaty hands, and heavy, tired arms because of all those push-ups, it was tough to maintain a grasp, and plenty of free kicks were given away. There was also no shortage of pairs getting tangled and falling into the dust. Great stuff for everyone else's amusement, but not so much fun for the embarrassed ones in the dirt. Megs was paired up with Matteo, and they began to find it was much easier when they talked to each other – simple things like 'left' or 'right', 'fast' or 'slow' made all the difference, and they began to take the game by the scruff of the neck.

Megs couldn't help but notice that Be and Catherine looked exhausted. They'd been OK in the volleying exercise, and had probably concentrated more than everyone else from the start because it wasn't an easy skill for them. But now they looked worn out.

'OK, OK. Stop. Good again. Not feel so stupid after a few minutes working together, no? Well done. Now, you just play game. Twenty minutes to go. I want full-paced game, but have some fun too. I want hard working and team working like we been training – but also, any time I see good trick, I award a point to that team. Goal is worth two points. But it must be useful trick that helps team, not trick just for hell of doing trick. Understand, Mr Megs?'

The Kids were tired, but it's easy to find a bit of extra zip when there's a game involved. So they picked the best bit of the ground to play on, and away they went.

The first point went to the Simpfenator – who was on Megs's team for this game. He did a lightning-fast stepover that sent Biscan completely the wrong way, setting up a great attacking move that Megs just missed finishing off.

Shortly after, though, something new was introduced to the Vootball Kids. Not a newly invented trick in itself, but something new for this group. And it was something Megs wasn't going to forget in a hurry.

The situation played out very quickly, but to Megs it was like being humiliated in slow motion. Paloma was on the opposite team to the Englishman for the first time in any of their practice matches, and she had taken her fine form from the Baystone game into this training session. She was wide on her attacking right wing, and shaped to receive a pass from Be, who hadn't been much involved in the game at all. In fact, Megs wondered whether it was a pass at all, or just a random attempt at a big kick that skewed off the side of her foot.

But, either way, the ball was heading to Paloma. It was bouncing awkwardly at about waist height on the uneven pitch, but she deftly took control on her thigh, just as Megs came running in to close down her space. Then, as the ball dropped towards the ground, she quickly flicked it back up to about head height as Megs's momentum took him flying just past her – and directly under the looping ball.

Megs immediately turned to get back at that ball. Paloma had hardly moved from the spot, and Megs was back on her case just as the ball bounced on the ground. In an almost exact replica of the previous manoeuvre, Paloma flicked the ball straight back up once again... and once again over the onrushing Englishman's head. Embarrassment and frustration burned in Megs's cheeks as Paloma deftly took control once more. Quickly she passed off to Abda a little further up the wing. Uncharacteristically she then stopped, turned to the now red-faced and puffing Englishman, raised her arms in the air, and cheered, 'SOMBRERO!!'

'Ha! Good, GOOD, good, Miss Paloma,' Atti laughed. 'I give you two points for two sombreros in one move! Very good. How that feel, Mr Megs?'

Mr Megs was fuming, and all the cheering wasn't helping. He bolted after the ball and laid a very heavy tackle on the hapless Catherine, which left them both on the ground - and made the ball fly way out of the pitch. Unfortunately for him, that just provided the excuse for everyone to laugh a bit more at his expense, and talk about the move Paloma had just made.

'What's it called?' Angelique asked.

'Sombrero. You know, like the big hats from Mexico or South America. The ones with massive brims and a kind of point on top.' Paloma gestured with a big sweep of her hands around her head. 'What d'ya think of it, Megs?'

Megs didn't want to think of anything except digging a little hole in the crusty ground and climbing in. Normally he was the one laughing at people after a trick, and he wasn't at all comfortable with this role reversal. Realising that no-one had gone after the ball, he saw his chance to get away from the unwanted attention, and ambled after it.

But as Megs mooched off, the Simpfenator couldn't resist the opportunity to tease. 'Come on, Megs – you did it to me with the nutmegs and thought it was funny. Get over yourself, man!' He was right, of course, but since when did that matter?

Atti was loving it, too. 'I first saw Puskas do sombrero in fifties. In fact, he did to me at my very first training with Honved. I was just boy and already very nervous, but he made me feel like infant. Maradona used to do it all time, too. Sombrero a good name, I always like it in English – over the head like big hat. Ha ha.'

By now, Megs had made his way back to the pitch, and his mood had lightened a bit. Swallowing his pride, he muttered a 'good one' to Paloma as the game started off again, then looked for Catherine so he could apologise for the fierceness of the tackle. But he was too late. Catherine had had enough, and was making her way back towards the school. Be was walking with her, the two of them casting long shadows as they went.

No more sombreros were completed in the remainder of the game, though plenty were attempted. Matteo managed to squeeze through an untidy nutmeg, but that was about it on the trick front.

Near the end of the match, Paloma had a clear chance to score what would've been the winner, and add to the quality of her evening's session. The intensity of the match had steadily heightened since the sombreros, and the tension was building when Abda shaped to cross from the left. Paloma was free in front of the goals, and the ball was perfectly delivered at head-height. For once, it looked like Paloma might let something above her shoulders actually connect with the ball... before she drew her head back in like a turtle and let the ball fly right by. The chance went begging along with the game – and it gave Megs plenty of ammunition to counter the fun she'd had earlier at his expense.

It was a good session, and Megs couldn't help but think that if they kept this up, they'd win the trip for sure. The Vootball Kids were flying.

Four | Home, Sweet Home

As the clock ticked past 7pm that night, Megs was becoming bored. His mum was bent over the glow of the computer, and his dad wasn't home from work yet. In fact, Megs hadn't seen Mr Morrison since the previous morning.

'When's Dad back?' he called.

'He's at work. Said he'd be late, but he can't be much longer now. Try his mobile if you like,' came the vague reply.

His mum seemed a bit grumpy lately, Megs reflected, and had reacted strangely when he'd come home and confirmed the news of the England trip. She'd shown far more concern than excitement, and Megs was hoping it'd be different when he told his dad. He wanted to share his big news face to face, not on the phone, so he let his mum's suggestion slide.

By 7.30pm there was still no sign of Mr Morrison, nor any sign of dinner. His mum hadn't budged from the keyboard, so Megs took action. 'Mum, what's for dinner? I'm starving.'

'Dinner? What time is it?' She checked her watch, which Megs didn't get since there was a clock on the computer screen. 'Seven-thirty!' she exclaimed. 'Where's your dad?'

'Dunno, that's what I asked you half-an-hour ago,' Megs replied with a grumpy edge to his voice. Hunger always shortened his fuse.

'Right, right. Uhmm... Why don't you walk down to that Thai place again and pick something up?' suggested Mrs Morrison. 'It's just around the corner, and there's some money in the freezer.'

'Huh?'

'The freezer,' explained his mum. 'It might seem stupid but – think about it - if anyone ever breaks in here, it's the last place they'll look. It's under the peas. Get whatever you like, but don't dilly-dally.'

Megs took out a frozen fifty-dollar note, holding it warily between finger and thumb. He shut the front door behind him with a bang, then headed off. He was puzzled about his dad, confused by his mum's attitude and altogether a bit worried.

Megs had already polished off his chicken satay starter, and was halfway through his green chicken curry main course when his dad nudged through the front door. Mrs Morrison was with her son on the couch by now and was trying to get her *Pad Thai* in the general vicinity of her mouth, determined to master the chopsticks.

Mr Morrison had his jacket slung over a bent arm and his tie loose around his neck. There were grey shadows under his eyes, and his hair was pushed back off his forehead. He attempted a smile and lamely joked, 'What is it with the Chinese and chopsticks? They invented gunpowder, built a massive wall that can be seen from the moon, and had an advanced civilisation centuries before most others, but they still can't get their heads around the idea that it's easier to eat rice with a fork than with two little sticks.'

'This is Thai food,' his wife replied sternly, as some ill-directed *Pad Thai* slopped back into her bowl.

Mr Morrison dumped his things where he stood, then collapsed between his family on the couch. 'Well, any Thai food for me then?'

'There's some lemongrass chicken and masaman curry over there,' Megs replied as he squeezed off the couch to fill his dad's plate. 'I've no idea what lemongrass is, and it's pretty obvious that Thai curries taste nothing like the Indian curries we're used to, but they're still pretty good.' From the corner of his eye, he saw his mum lean over and give his old man a kiss on the forehead.

'Where've you been, Dad? Working late?' Megs asked.

'Unfortunately, yes. And it looks like I'll be doing it for a while, too. And I'll have to do some travelling in the next few weeks. How do you say it... it's "full on dot com" at the moment.' He sighed.

'What do you mean, travelling?' Mrs Morrison asked suspiciously.

But Megs got in before his dad could reply, skipping around his mum's concern on the way. 'Yeah! Full on dot com forward-slash crazy, I'd say. Hey, dad – you'll never guess what I found out today.' In his excitement, Megs let the curry slop into his dad's bowl far too quickly, and a fair portion of it ended up on the table where he was serving. Luckily, his parents were looking the other way and didn't see the mess he was making. He quickly scooped the spilt curry back into the bowl.

'Doesn't have something to do with winning the Championship with the Down Under Wanderers, does it?' smiled Mr Morrison. 'A little birdy whispered something about something to do with the winners going somewhere we know pretty well. Am I on the right track?'

Megs stared at his dad in surprise.

'I might be flat out at work, but your mum and I still speak, you know.'

Megs's moment had been ruined again. But even that couldn't keep him down. 'Well, it was all confirmed at training today. How cool is it? Going back to England, a chance to see the guys again, and even maybe play Liverpool. I wonder if they'll let us play at Anfield.' Megs was babbling. 'How incredible would that be? Still, I'd be happy just to play at Melwood. Who knows who we'd see about the place – maybe Stevie Gerrard would come over and watch us when the first team finished training? Maybe we can organise a game of the Wendesley Wanderers against the Down Under Wanderers...'

'I agree, it's a fantastic opportunity,' cut in his dad.

'But first you have to win the whole championship in your team's first season, and even though you won your first game at a canter, a championship is a marathon, not a sprint. You know that. So don't get your hopes up too high just yet.'

Megs didn't reply. He handed his dad his dinner (complete with chopsticks for a laugh), then settled back into the couch to finish his own food with one eye on the randomly chosen TV show. His parents might not be so convinced, but Megs was sure the team would win the trip. They had to. They just had to.

Five | Happiness Is Where the Heart Is

Hi Lads,

Well, it's true. The winner of the title this year will win a trip to England. All that stuff I emailed to you guys the other day is true. Can you believe it? It'll be weird playing against you guys if we get the trip, and you'll see how good some of our girls are.

Mum and Dad don't seem too excited about it though. In fact, they don't seem too excited about anything at the moment. Don't know what's going on there.

Anyway, write back, you lazy sods. This is a big bloody deal!

Megs

Megs didn't want to seem too desperate about his friends not writing back to him, but the truth was that he was a bit put out. It'd only been a couple of days, but surely this was big enough news to get them typing! Especially for Woody, who was having a trip to Australia with his dad in a couple of months.

Megs was finding himself less and less bothered about

putting much detail into his emails back home. It was too hard to explain properly how things were going in his new home, and it seemed like the lads in his old town were losing interest a bit anyway. They spoke on the phone occasionally when they got the times right, but even though they all had Skype or iChat, they'd only used it once when Stevie R had called through to Megs. Thing was, because Stevie thought he was a hip-hop gangster, the way he spoke made things tough enough at the best of times, and coupled with a bad Skype connection, Megs couldn't make head or tail of what he was saying. It has been a bit weird, to be honest.

It was too dark for a kick, and things were increasingly quiet and boring around the house. His dad was working late again and his mum seemed a bit tense, so after he had pressed 'Send' on the email, he figured he might as well get some homework out of the way.

Megs was just finishing off his 'Around Australia Car Rally' assignment, and he had to admit he was pretty into it. Most of the time he didn't know he was actually doing homework, as he transported himself off to find out about all the new places. By now, the dodgy old 4WD he'd bought at the start had fallen in a heap and died. It hadn't been his idea, but Miss Sheather had made it happen, and she was the boss of the game. 'That's life,' she'd said. 'Now you have to figure out what to do.' Megs had figured that paying out for airfares might be a better way to go than buying a new car at this late stage of the game. Why not finish the trip in style? He had the money in his 'bank', he reasoned, so it was aeroplanes, tours and rockstar-quality hotels from here on in. In the real world, he'd love to be able to do the same one day.

The school assignment had taken him all the way up the east coast of Australia, across the Northern Territory and down the West Coast. In the real world, he thought, there'd be no way the beaten-up old car he'd bought would've made it that far, but Miss Sheather was being kind to him, seeing as he was new to the school, and Megs was happy to make the most of it.

His fictional self was currently in Perth, and planning to take the boat down the Swan River to Fremantle, where he decided he'd spend some of his remaining make-believe money on a five-star hotel and some world-famous West Australian seafood. He discovered that Fremantle is near the place where the first Europeans landed in Australia – way before Captain Cook and his English fleet. Some Dutch and Portuguese ships had got lost and bumped into the southern tip of Western Australia in the early 1600s.

Apparently a Dutchman called Dirk Hartog was the first guy to land. It was 1616, and it was on an island just off the western coast of the mainland. He inscribed a pewter plate and nailed it to a post, then moved on. That area is now called Cape Inscription, and there is a Dirk Hartog Island as well.

These early explorers had stayed for a bit, Megs discovered, but decided the land wasn't worth anything and they should probably get going and try to find their way again. They had no idea what they'd landed on, because no-one had ever mapped it.

Part of a Portuguese ship was even found on the beach not far from Fremantle, and there are people who constantly search the sand dunes for a ship believed to have been abandoned in the area. It sounded like a cool treasure hunt to Megs, and he took a mental note. Maybe he could badger his mum and dad to take their next family holiday in Western Australia so that he could join in the fun…

Finally, Megs researched the cost of a business-class flight from Perth to Adelaide in South Australia, and decided to include it in his budget. He updated his itinerary to include two more nights in the five-star Fremantle hotel, and noted in his diary all the things he'd discovered. He was keeping his budget in an Excel spreadsheet, and enjoyed watching all the numbers change when he added in his new costs.

By the time that was all done, it was nearing 9.30pm, and his dad still wasn't home. His mum was sprawled on the couch sleeping in front of the television. Not wanting to wake her, Megs went off quietly to his room, then reached for his iPod and flicked through a few old editions of *Shoot* before settling down to sleep.

It used to be that school was the lonely place, not home.

Megs woke sometime in the middle of the night to the sound of his parents arguing. He couldn't make out every word, but enough came through the walls to give him the idea that his mum wasn't at all happy about his dad being away so much. He heard the word 'Australia' mentioned quite a bit, too, but couldn't figure out what a country could've done wrong. Yeah, it'd got in the way of a few Portuguese ships a long time ago, but that couldn't be what his parents were arguing about.

His dad worked hard, Megs knew that. But he missed him being around, and guessed his mum did too. Whatever the problem was, he hated hearing his parents like this, so tried to block it out of his mind. He put his pillow over his head, then put his fingers in his ears (stopped the noise, but made it impossible to sleep). Finally, he reached for his trusty iPod and that did the trick – but only once he'd put on the kind of classical music that his mum listened to when gardening. It was calm, and so boring that it helped Megs to finally nod off.

Next morning the house was quiet, but as Megs poured himself some breakfast cereal, he noticed a note on the table.

Morning Megs,

Sorry I didn't see you last night. Or the last few mornings. Work's been frantic. I have to go away tomorrow for a week, but I'll be home to see you tonight. Maybe we can have a kick if you're not too tired after the game – Mum tells me something about a trick called a 'sunhat' or 'pinata' or something. You'll have to show me. Have a great game!

Love, Dad.

The heaviness lifted a little, and Megs began shovelling in his breakfast with growing enthusiasm. After all, it was match day!

The paper was on the table next to him, open at the sports pages. His dad must have spent some time with it this morning, too.

Most of the news covered 'the rugbies' as his mum called them, as well as international swimming and horse racing. There were snippets of news about the real football, but it was all 'In Brief' and nothing new to anyone who used the internet. There was, however, one little football piece that did catch Megs's eye.

GIRL, 11, BANNED
FOR WEARING HIJAB

Quebec soccer officials would uphold a young girl's expulsion from a tournament for wearing a hijab, they said, unless FIFA changes gear rules.

Asmahan Mansour, 11, was ousted from a tournament for refusing to take off her hijab, the head scarf worn by many Muslim women for religious reasons.

Brigette Frot, executive director of the Quebec Soccer Federation, said Mansour was not allowed to take the field for safety reasons, not religious objections, declaring: *'It's unfortunate. I believe FIFA will have to rule yes or no, whether hijabs are permitted on the soccer field. Whatever they decide, we'll abide by the rules.'*

Reports said the referee, who is Muslim himself, feared Mansour could be choked if players tugged on the scarf.

'Following FIFA rules, the referee asked the young girl to remove her hijab, fearing it posed a danger to her and other players. She refused,' Frot said.

Mansour's team quit the tournament. Four other teams joined the boycott.

Huh. Abda wears a headscarf, Megs thought to himself. In fact, Megs didn't even know what colour hair she had. Black, probably, he imagined.

A knock on the door interrupted Megs's thoughts. Paloma was early. He asked her in while he got his bags sorted, then poked his head into his mum's room, and, not knowing if she was still asleep, said a quiet goodbye. No shower, no brushed teeth and no breakfast plates put away.

'Why's your bag so big?' Paloma asked once they'd left the house.

'Change of boots, kit, warm-up top, shin pads, drink bottle, towel, runners, flip-flops. You have to be prepared.'

'People don't get that prepared for holidays!' Paloma giggled as she held open her 'Go Green' supermarket shopping bag. 'You should have wheels on that bag of yours,' she continued. 'You'll be even shorter by the time we get to school!'

Megs was appalled as he glanced into Paloma's 'sports

bag'. Mr Mac back in England would've been horrified. Everything was crammed in all higgledy-piggledy on top of each other, dirty boots rubbing against the clean new Pennendale Wanderers kit.

'What... that's it?' Megs was amazed. 'Surely you should respect your kit a bit more than that!'

'Whatever! Let's see if it makes any difference to how I play,' laughed Paloma. 'And at least I won't get injured before the game by carrying this around!' She swung her little shopping bag high above her head.

Megs trudged on beside her, schoolbag looped onto one shoulder and sports bag slung over the other.

'And by the way,' Paloma continued, 'what the hell is a flip-flop?'

Megs looked at Paloma warily, waiting to be made fun of. 'You know – summer sandals. Everyone wears them here. At the beach and all that. Flip-flops.'

Paloma screwed up her face. She obviously didn't get it, so Megs stopped, dropped his bag with a thud, and opened it. Everything was neatly folded and placed into compartments. It positively sparkled, and there was no way his boots (either pair) were going to touch his kit – no need to bring on any bad luck before a match.

'Whoa... look at that!' Paloma laughed. 'You have a room as messy as mine, but this bag is like a hospital ward. I'm surprised there aren't roses and lavender in there to keep it smelling nice!'

'There's nothing wrong with feeling like a professional. Look and feel like a player, and you're halfway to becoming a player. That's what Mr Mac used to say.'

Megs sounded prim.

'Funny – I would've thought if you play well and score goals, then you actually are a player. You can't play in your bag, you know!' Paloma was on a roll.

'You do it your way, and I'll do it mine. Anyway…' Megs said triumphantly, pulling something out of the left hand zip compartment. 'Here's the flip-flop. Surely you can't make fun of that!'

'This is what you call a flip-flop? That's a thong!' laughed Paloma. Seemed Megs was wrong – Paloma *could* make fun of it.

'More to the point – why do you call it a thong?' retorted Megs. 'You know what a thong is, don't you?'

'What d'you mean?' asked Paloma, subdued for once.

'A thong is… well…' Megs blushed. What on earth was he doing having this conversation? Still, he'd come too far to turn back now. He took a deep breath, then continued, 'It's that bit of ladies' underwear that – you know – doesn't go over all of your bum,' Megs replied as a he gestured rather awkwardly down the middle of his backside.

'That's called a g-string, isn't it? Who calls it a thong?' asked a bewildered Paloma.

'That's what they call it in England, and I'm pretty sure in America, too,' Megs replied, happy to be over the worst of the conversation. 'You've seen MTV… there was that song about it.'

'So hang on,' Paloma said slowly, 'a g-string is a thong, and a thong is a…'

'… flip-flop.'

'And why is it a flip-flop?'

'Dunno. Because of the sound they make when you walk, I guess.'

'Come to think of it, you're probably right on that one. Flip-flop does make a bit more sense,' Paloma conceded as Megs tucked his 'thongs' back where they belonged, and they headed off again.

'So what d'you think Roverdale will be like this arvo?' Megs asked.

'I've heard they've got some good players. There's a couple of Spanish guys I know from some social things I have to go to with my parents, and I know they play for clubs as well as school. They were in the top few teams in last year's comp. Like Atti said, we can't expect to win 5–0 every week.'

'Is their school far?'

'Nah – a short bus-ride. But I don't know if you and that bag will both fit on…'

As they approached the school, Megs looked towards the main building. It was a grand-looking thing. Rather English, he always felt, like a link back to his old life. Somehow, it was quite comforting.

When he looked this morning, however, he did a double-take. The building was the same, but what was sitting next to it wasn't.

The Morrison family car was in the visitors' carpark.

Throughout the morning, Megs found it difficult to concentrate on his schoolwork. Had he done something wrong? He was doing OK at school, and ever since his 'day off' a couple of months ago, he hadn't been in any serious trouble.

And was it his mum or his dad at the school? When he'd left home, his mum had been asleep and his dad had taken the car to work. It had to be his dad. But he was at work. Did his mum know Dad was here?

By recess time the car was gone but Megs's curiosity remained. He toyed with the idea of going to the office and asking if his dad had visited, but maybe it wasn't really their car. It probably wasn't really any of his business either, or they would've told him.

Val broke into his thoughts.

'All primed for this afternoon?' she asked, her notebook at the ready.

'Huh?' said Megs, snapping to attention. 'Oh, yeah, sorry. Hi Val. What…? You're interviewing people before games as well, now? You're really getting into this, aren't you?'

Ignoring the comment, Val pushed on. 'You scored three goals last week against Baystone. How many can we expect this week?'

Megs had watched enough TV interviews to know how to answer that one. 'Well, I can only hope the team wins. It doesn't matter how many I score.' Secretly, he wanted to score two.

'And do you think you will win?'

'Well, we've been training hard and Atti's been doing a great job. I think we have every chance of winning.' A great TV interview response – but really, the answer in his mind was: *Hell, yeah, I reckon we'll kill 'em.*

'And how have you settled into playing in Australia?'

Good question, Megs thought. TV response: 'Very well, I think. Everybody has been great to me, and I'm enjoying it. We have some really good players who could play back in England, no problems.'

Response in head: *Being on the other side of the planet is damn tough and sometimes it's really lonely. The lads back there are emailing me less and less, and my parents are arguing. I hardly see my dad any more, and my mum is either quietly working on the computer or asleep somewhere. Playing football and thinking about football is the best bit about living here. Who would've guessed that, all those months ago when my parents decided to move Down Under!*

'And finally, Megs, do you think Pennendale will win the Championship and the trip to England?'

TV response: 'Well, we just have to take one game at a time and see what happens.'

Response in head: *Yeah, we'll win it! We'll go back to England, we'll show the teams over there what we're made of, and I'll catch up with all my friends just like it used to be. I'll meet Steven Gerrard at Liverpool's Melwood training ground and we'll have a kick together. Oh – and I'll nutmeg him for good measure as well.*

Val jotted down the final TV response, gave Megs a professional nod of the head and a thank you before zipping off to catch Matteo. Over her shoulder, she called out to Megs, 'Kick hard and run fast!'

Kick hard and run fast indeed. Roverdale Primary School watch out!

Six | Closer to England

The game against Roverdale started well – very well, in fact.

Matteo was captain for the day (Atti liked to share the responsibility around) and won the toss.

Paloma took the kick-off by passing it short to Abda. But instead of the next pass going backwards to the central midfielder, like you usually see, Abda turned and immediately dribbled forward. Biscan was prepared wide on the left wing, supported by the Simpfenator. Abda quickly sent the ball in their direction, and the Wanderers were immediately on the attack.

Biscan took control, drew in a defender, then passed the ball further down the wing as the Simpfenator overlapped. With excellent control for a big player, the Simpfenator took one touch to lay it in front of himself. At full pace, he approached the edge of the box. Without messing about, he immediately swung his leg to cross the ball deep into the danger area. Roverdale were back-pedalling under the razor-sharp onslaught, and Pennendale were streaming forward in a sea of blue.

The cross was expertly delivered, and Abda, Megs, Paloma and Danny were all fully prepared for this passage of play. Megs was closest to the dropping ball, and threw himself bravely into its path as the opposing goalkeeper came off his line to punch it clear. Under Megs's pressure, the keeper missed the ball (and only just missed knocking Megs's head clean off his shoulders) and they fell to the ground in a tangled heap.

The ball bounced clear to Paloma, who tried to control it under pressure from the retreating defence. She probably should've tried to hit it first time, as the delay allowed the defender to poke the ball away.

The keeper was quickly making his way to his feet, but Abda was on top of it. She pounced on the disputed ball, spun on her left leg at an awkward height, and did all she could to connect her right foot to the ball. It wasn't pretty, but nevertheless the ball edged back towards the goal. The keeper made a desperate effort to get back as the ball trickled towards the goal-line.

Slowly it rolled; quickly he ran. The ball slowed; the keeper sped up.

But despite the keeper's final, desperate lunge, the ball ever so gently rolled over the line. It was going so slowly it didn't even hit the back of the net, but a goal is a goal, and it was 1–0 to Pennendale!

Atti clapped to himself on the sidelines as his players went bananas, content that the hard work on the training ground had paid off.

Roverdale kicked off, a little shell-shocked by Pennendale's frantic start to the game. And they weren't about to let up. As Atti had drilled into them, immediately following any restart is a good time to pressure like crazy and try to get the ball back.

Full of beans after such a perfect start, the Pennendale players swarmed over their opposition, putting them under enough pressure that their left midfielder hurriedly kicked the ball clear of their half to avoid being tackled. It was easy pickings for Matteo, who calmly took control of the ball, got his head up, and passed off to another team-mate. Pennendale was on the attack again.

Val was on the sideline, madly writing notes, her pen moving almost as fast as her friends in the Pennendale blue. She was even more impressed when, after ten minutes, Paloma crashed one home from just inside the box; 2–0 and flying!

Twenty-three minutes later, it was 3–0 after an ambitious shot from outside the box by Megs took a nasty deflection that totally wrong-footed the hapless Roverdale keeper. What a day he was having!

At the other end of the pitch, Max was becoming bored in the Pennendale goal. The only thing he had had to do was clear a back-pass from Matteo, but he was keeping himself involved by calling out plenty of encouragment to his team-mates in front of him. By the time the half-time whistle blew, he'd only had to make one simple save, and the Pennendale side strolled off to the break, all smiles and confidence.

'Good, good. You do good and we winning well. Very well. I make some substitutions to make sure everyone play, but the big thing now is that you don't stop to play.

You scored three goal, and it could have been ten. That mean possible for other team to do same. Don't be nice to them – next half must be just like first half.'

Atti's words were to echo throughout the second half – because his team did the opposite. They stopped doing what they'd been doing so well in the first half, and their earlier concentration and commitment turned into sloppiness. They allowed the opposition back into the game, and gradually, Max became the busier of the two keepers.

Thirty-two minutes into the half, Roverdale was awarded a penalty after a lazy, reckless tackle from Seb brought down the opposing striker. The penalty strike was excellent – right into the bottom corner, giving Max no hope. The score was 3–1 with thirteen minutes left.

Roverdale had their confidence back, and began battering the Pennendale goal. The Wanderers just couldn't get out of their own half and, if not for some desperate defending from Matteo, Angelique, Biscan and Max, the team would've slipped further into trouble. Atti kept looking at his watch, as if willing time to go faster.

With three minutes to go, Roverdale snatched a well-deserved second goal. Danny was guilty of over-playing too close to his own goal when he should've passed or cleared the ball; he turned with the ball right into trouble and was dispossessed by two defenders. Roverdale were in an easy position to score, and did just that. Problems were brewing for the team in blue.

But they hung on – though only after the crossbar saved them in the last minute. Another three points could be added to their list, but not without some serious stress!

Atti was fuming after the game, but gave himself a few minutes to calm down before addressing his squad.

'OK, OK, we win, so I happy. But phew!' he cried out as he slapped his forehead. 'You people nearly give me heart attacking!' Slowly he shook his head, looking from one face to the next, then continued seriously: 'I keep it short, but I have lesson to teach you. Thing is, when play vootball, don't think of score. Same with everything, really. Score look after itself.'

Megs was confused… how could you not think of the score? What was the point of playing without a score?

'I don't mean don't want to win.' Atti could tell he wasn't getting through to them. 'What I mean is, if every player keep doing their job, and keep doing things right, moment by moment, score will look after itself. Worry about score after game, but during game just keep doing everything to your best at every moment. Today we not do that. Today we thought we won at half-time, so we stopped doing things right, and starting hoping about the score. We lucky, because we win anyway. So good, but think of the lesson.' He turned abruptly. 'See you on bus.'

What Atti said made sense and, judging from the rate at which Val had been scribbling notes, Megs had the feeling they'd be reminded of Atti's words in the next match report. The Wanderers were out of jail on this one, but they were still sitting pretty on six points from six, and that was worth being happy about. Before long, a high five from Matteo confirmed Megs's thoughts.

ROUND 5				
CLUB	W	L	D	Pts
Southside Sharks	**4**	**0**	**1**	**13**
Pennendale Wanderers	4	0	1	13
Penders Grove	4	0	1	13

Over the next few weeks, the Wanderers went from strength to strength. The players were developing an excellent understanding of each other and, after five games, had had four wins and a draw. They were equal on points with Penders Grove and Southside Sharks, but Southside was leading the way on goal difference. Megs never had liked sharks, and was looking forward to playing them in a couple of weeks.

On the flip-side, however, things were becoming increasingly tense at home. The atmosphere was doing Megs's head in, and something had to give. Then one Wednesday evening after training, it happened.

The pressure valve burst.

Seven | Even Closer to England Than He Thought

That Wednesday's session was another good one, and Megs had felt light on his feet. But by the time he made it home and left Paloma to walk on, his mood had flipped. His mum and dad were arguing again. He could hear them before he'd even opened the door.

As he reached for the scratched brass knob to let himself in, something stopped him, and he slumped onto the doorstep instead. Immediately, he wished he was back at training.

The argument from inside continued for a good five minutes, and Megs's bum was starting to go numb from the cold concrete. His jaw was getting sore from grinding his teeth – the muscles working overtime without his even knowing it.

He'd had enough of this rubbish. It was too much. Angrily, he picked up his bag, spun around, and headed towards the street. He didn't know where he was going, but he walked purposefully anyway. When he made it to the nature strip outside the gate, he looked left, then right, then sat down on the kerb. At least he couldn't hear his parents from this distance.

Picking up a deformed-looking stick, he began drawing aimless patterns in a band of dirt in the gutter.

I bet Paloma is having a great time with her family, and here I am in the gutter, he thought as he bashed the end of the stick into the concrete. And that's when he decided. *Stuff it.* Why should he have to sit in the gutter? It was his house too! Time for Megs to do what he had to do.

Springing to his feet, he grabbed his bag, and headed back to the front door. The voices were still loud, but not as bad as before. Without a second's thought, he opened the front door with as much vigour as possible, making sure that it crashed against the inside wall. Maybe it would even make a hole in the plaster.

His mum and dad both swung their heads in the direction of their angry son. Immediately there was silence.

Still upset, and encouraged by the success of his entrance, Megs powered on.

'Right,' he announced. 'I've had enough. For weeks now you've been arguing. *You've* either been sleeping or on the computer, and *you've* hardly ever been here.' He pointed at each of his parents in turn. 'It used to be school I didn't want to go to, but now it's home. Do you realise I've been sitting out in the gutter, not even wanting to come into the house? Is it my fault?'

Mr and Mrs Morrison looked at their son in silence. And then he went for it. 'Are you going to get divorced?' He knew it happened a lot, but until he actually said it, he hadn't thought it was a possibility for his parents. And now that the words were out of his mouth, he began to panic that it might actually be true.

Megs's arms were crossed stubbornly in front of his chest, and his mouth was puckered into a little ball. He was fighting back tears as the emotion of his outburst started to take over.

His mum spoke first, and seemed more 'normal' than Megs had seen her in weeks – like a switch had been flicked in her head.

'Edward, honey, what are you talking about? We aren't getting divorced! Come here…' As she approached Megs with open arms and drew him close, he could see tears brimming in her eyes. It felt good to be hugged, but Megs wanted to stay angry. He squirmed out of his mother's arms.

Mr Morrison's cheeks were flushed, and he took a step forward, extending a helpless hand. 'Whoa! You look fit to pop! How long have you felt like this?'

More calmly now, though proud of his earlier effort, Megs tried to explain. 'It feels like I've been by myself in this house for ages, and I want to know what's going on. Everything is weird and I don't get it.'

Mr Morrison sat down on the arm of a chair and spoke calmly, but his eyes were shinier than usual. 'You know how, when we first arrived, you struggled to fit in? Well, adults often feel the same way, too. It's been tough for us lately – and especially for your mum. We should probably have talked to you about it long ago.'

Megs sat down on the couch and after a minute his

mother came and sat beside him. This time he didn't shy away from her hug. Then they talked. Well, two of them talked, and Megs listened. It was always a bit uncomfortable to have 'serious chats' with his parents, and he never knew where to look. He wished his football was close by so he could roll it around under his feet as they spoke. Without it, he found himself picking at the skin on the side of his fingernails, especially around his thumbs.

Over the next hour or so, Megs discovered that the tension in their lives could be traced back to that unexpected visit by Mr Braithwaite several weeks ago. He had come to tell Mr Morrison that Braithwaite Machine Tools had lost their major client, and that Mr Morrison would have to do some extra travelling around Australia and Asia to help revive the company's fortunes. Either that, or he would have to be 'let go' and face unemployment. The company was unable to offer more money at this stage, so Mr Morrison had had to make a tough choice.

'Not that I really had much of a choice,' he explained to Megs, 'in a new land with no contacts or referees... so I accepted the extra workload and hoped for the best.'

Megs heaved a sigh of relief. At least the problem was nothing to do with him. And his parents weren't about to get divorced.

'The news really rocked our confidence.' Megs's mother took up the story. 'But we tried to keep it from you – which was silly, I suppose. You were settling down so happily...'

Mr Morrison spoke briskly, as though to get everything

out in the open at last. 'We even talked about moving back to England. I thought it might be better for your mother than being alone all day. I didn't know whether we could afford to take a risk on a company that seemed to be on the skids.'

Megs found his voice. 'I wish you hadn't tried to spare me,' he told them.

Mr Morrison nodded soberly. 'I guess we can't protect you from everything.'

'And that's the reason we weren't so excited about the trip your team could win back to England.' It was Mrs Morrison's turn. 'One problem is that we could be living back there by then, and the other is that if we are still living here, we probably won't be able to pay for anything like that.' She patted Megs's shoulder apologetically. 'So we felt pressured from all sides.'

'Thing is,' Megs replied, 'I don't want to go back. Maybe that's a surprise after my bad start, but I've made friends and I like it here better than over there.' The words felt strange coming out of his own mouth, but Megs knew they were starting to become true. 'It was you two who said we have to give it a really good go and that it'd be tough at the start. We've only been here four and a half months, so surely that's still the start, isn't it? You can't tell me one thing, then do something else yourselves. And we can worry about paying for the trip later, can't we? I think some of it's sponsored anyway.'

A slight smile flickered across Mrs Morrison's face as she glanced at her husband. 'He's your son, isn't he!' she said. Then, turning to Megs, 'Your dad has been saying that for the last fortnight, but I just don't know…' She turned to face her son. 'Sorry, Megs, I guess we've been pretty selfish, and I'm glad you let us know. We should thank you for that.'

'I know!' It came to Megs in a flash, and he jolted up from his slump on the couch. 'Let's get that dog! That'll help you with homesickness, won't it? I asked before, and you said maybe. Well? Can we? Pleeeaasse…'

'Since when do you like dogs?' Mr Morrison interrupted.

'Since we have enough room for one! Come on, Mum.' Megs was suddenly determined. 'It'll be cute as, and it'll help keep you company as well. We can call it Anfield to remind us of home!' Megs was getting good at pushing all the right buttons to get his own way.

'Actually, it's not a bad idea, Jenny. Not bad at all. You've always loved animals.' Mr Morrison was on board.

'We'll see,' Mrs Morrison said slowly. 'But you might be right. Maybe it'd help.'

'So we're staying then?' Megs needed some confirmation. After he'd made all that effort, made new friends, got a coach, formed a team (who were undefeated for the past five games!) – they couldn't give up now. Not yet! The stress was making him bite his nails.

'Yes… we're staying,' answered Mrs Morrison, almost reluctantly. 'But that doesn't mean you don't have to help me fix that hole you smashed in the wall earlier, by the way. And a lot depends on how the job goes. With less money, we're obviously going to struggle, but I guess we can take a risk on Vincent for a little while longer.'

Megs felt a surge of happiness. 'Oh, and another thing. Did you guys come up to the school the other day? Did I see your car?'

'Wow, there's no keeping anything from you, is there?' Mr Morrison was impressed. 'Yes, I went along to talk to them about how you're going. It's not like we've forgotten all about you, you know. We wanted to know if you were settling in at school now, and it seems you definitely are.'

'What's for dinner?' Megs asked, changing the topic.

'It'll have to be bangers and mash.' Mrs Morrison headed for the kitchen.

Megs went to his room and juggled, bouncing the ball in quick succession on his right foot as he stood dead still on his left. Then he pulled out his chair, some books and whatever else was lying around in his room, and practised dribbling... megsing the chair at least nine times before his mother called him to the table.

Eight | Two Homes Are Better Than One

'Oh... he'll be devastated. I am too. Uh-huh. Yes, yes. I know. It's such a long way – I've been really feeling that lately. Yes. So is there a chance for later? Hmmm. I see.'

Mrs Morrison was on the phone early that next weekend, and didn't sound too upbeat. At least she was out of bed though, Megs noted, as he came into the kitchen. She did seem a bit more cheerful the last few days.

'Look, he's up now,' his mother concluded, glumly. 'They might as well talk about it themselves, I suppose.' She held the handset out to Megs.

'Hello,' he muttered uncertainly into the phone.

'Megs. That you?' came the voice down the line. An English voice.

'Yeah... who's this?' Megs was a bit uncomfortable. He hated it when callers expected you to guess who they were.

'*Who's this?* What d'ya mean, man? I know it's been a while, but who d'ya think?' It wasn't an adult voice.

'Sounds like a Reds man to me!' Megs replied, rapidly

getting excited. 'Is that you, Woody?'

'Sure is. You don't sound Aussie yet. Good stuff. Can't have that.'

'Funny though – you sound more Scouser.' Megs suddenly felt a bit homesick for the sounds of his old home.

'How's it all going? We've not been in touch for a while, huh?' Woody sounded genuinely interested, even though Megs hadn't heard from any of his crew back in England in weeks and weeks.

'Pretty well. We're settling in pretty well.' What could he say? How could he tell him everything? It was a bit like the responses to Val's interview the other week. It's often easier to tell people what they want to hear even though deep down, he wanted to spill his beans.

'Things are all the same over here. Stevie R is still confusing everyone, and is talking about getting a tattoo. Can you believe it!? Got his ear pierced the other day – but a tattoo!'

'As if anyone'd do it! He's only eleven!'

'Twelve now. Was his birthday the other day. But he reckons he knows someone who'd do it. You know what he's like!' Woody laughed.

'What a tool! What did you all do for the day?' *I missed his birthday...*

'It was good, actually. Went bowling. There's some cool bowling places now, with games consoles as well as the bowling. Even the stupid bowling shoes are cool. Stevie insisted on using one of those ramp things to send his ball down instead of bowling it. Said it was his birthday, he could do what he wanted.'

I missed his birthday. Megs felt hollow.

'The next day we all went to see the boys play Wigan. It was only Wigan, but Anfield is Anfield, huh, and the Reds are the Reds. We didn't go to celebrate Stevie's birthday, but of course he thought we did. Dan had to tell him to shut it all day! Mr Mac got us tickets, and we all went. We won, of course, and Gerrard was brilliant. We even got to go into the players' tunnel and onto the pitch after the match. It was SO COOL. Funny how quiet the stadium was after the match. Just us and the birds, but you'd swear you could still see the players running around out there and hear the crowd. Like ghosts or something. And that grass... man, that grass. That pitch is like it's been painted, it's so green.'

If he felt hollow before, Megs was positively empty now. Woody was talking at a million miles an hour, but Megs didn't mind. *What else have I missed?* he wondered.

'So how's things? Sorry I haven't replied to many emails, man. Things seem to be going pretty well though. Do you reckon you'll win the League and get to come home? Sounds like you've had a good start.'

And Megs finally opened up. The League, his team, his friends, the competition – everything except what was going on with his parents. He talked. And talked. The minutes sped away, but Megs was oblivious to that, and was starting to feel pretty great. His discomfort was gone, he was on a roll. It was like the old days.

'So your mum hasn't told you?' Woody interrupted.

Megs dried up in mid-sentence. 'Told me what?'

'That I'm not coming out anymore,' came the reply.

Megs's heart dropped. He'd forgotten all about Woody's trip. He whispered, 'What d'ya mean?'

'Well, Dad's conference isn't on anymore, so he doesn't have to come for work. I've tried to get 'em to let me come by myself, but they aren't interested. It is a long way, I s'pose.'

Megs was shocked. He hadn't really talked with anyone about Woody coming, but now that he knew it wasn't going to happen, he realised how much he actually wanted him to. And his mum and dad must've felt just the same. They were friends with Woody's parents, too.

'So is there any chance? Have you tried everything?' Megs asked, feeling a bit desperate.

'Yeah, I've done everything, sorry to say. The conference might be on again later in the year, but I've tried everything. It's a no, man. Sorry.'

Megs felt like one of those balloons where all the air comes back out before you tie it off properly. Like he was zipping uncontrollably around the room. He felt a long way from anywhere.

'Well, that's a massive bummer, I've gotta say.' Megs had to force himself to sound normal. 'It was gonna be so cool.'

'You'll just have to win that League of yours, and get yourself over here. Which Wanderers will you play for when that happens? The yellow and black or that rubbish blue you have to wear over there?' Woody was obviously trying to lighten the mood again.

Megs followed his lead and continued, 'Maybe half

each. And own goals at either end. What d'ya think?'

But they couldn't get back the zest of the earlier conversation. Megs felt funny. Just minutes before, it'd seemed like the old days, but now he knew that was only the memory of those old days. These days were different. He was obviously upset his friend wasn't coming to visit anymore, but that wasn't why he felt funny. The strange thing was that he'd fully processed the news, yet he wasn't actually as upset as he thought he should be. Not as devastated as his mum was expecting.

Woody and Megs said their farewells and good lucks and promised to keep in touch better. Megs hung up the phone on his side of the planet as Woody did the same on his. Even though he was acutely aware of that distance, Megs felt strangely content about it all. Accepting. And maybe a small part of him was even happy to keep Australia and his Pennendale Wanderers apart from Liverpool and the Wendesley Wanderers.

'You OK, honey?' his mum asked tentatively. She obviously feared the news might be too much for him after his last few anxious weeks.

'I am, actually. Weird.' With that, Megs turned on his heels, headed for the kitchen with a cheerful smile and poured himself a gigantic bowl of Weet-bix. When he dunked his spoon in, some milk escaped over the edge.

His bucket of breakfast finished, Megs turned his attention to the computer. Not for homework (it was Sunday morning, after all), but to check emails. With so much going on lately, it'd been a while since he'd been online.

The first one he opened was from Val and was titled 'Top of the Table Clash'.

Top of the Table Clash

This Friday afternoon, Southside Sharks and Pennendale Wanderers will do battle to mark the end of the first round of matches in this year's Western Region competition. The clash will be a major test of both teams' aspirations to win the League and thereby claim the trip to England.

Megs felt his heart flutter as he read on.

Currently, the Sharks top the table, undefeated with 23 points. Pennendale Wanderers are next, three points behind after their narrow loss to Thornbury two weeks ago. Next come the Rockets on 18 points after recently winning three straight, followed by early pace-setters Penders Grove.

ROUND 8				
CLUB	W	L	D	Pts
Southside Sharks	6	0	2	20
Pennendale Wanderers	5	1	2	17
Hills Rockets	4	1	3	15
Penders Grove	4	2	2	14

Pennendale have only lost once so far this season, and will be looking to keep in touch with the League leaders with another win this week.

The Sharks are the only undefeated team and are building a reputation for being ruthless and fierce in the tackle. Their strength lies in their strength, and the Pennendale coach Atti Czibar has been plotting ways to use his team's pace, teamwork and fast ball movement to snatch this game.

Don't give away all our secrets, Val! Megs thought.

The only injury concern for either team is Pennendale's Biscan Mihlalovic who twisted his ankle during a lunchtime kick-about while trying to perfect a double-sombrero.

Using the right language, and all! You're really into this! Megs was impressed.

Both teams love to attack, so there promises to be plenty of action, and we hope there will be a big crowd on hand to play their part. The match will be played at the Sharks' home ground in the new Southside Estate and will kick off at 4pm this Monday.

The full match report will be available on the school's website on Tuesday.

Val did a great job of remaining 'neutral' when she was reporting, even though Megs knew she was dying for Pennendale to win the match and draw level with the Sharks on the leader board. At training, everyone had been talking about how Southside just booted the ball long all the time and relied on their individual strength to win matches. The Pennendale defenders were going to have their work cut out, but Atti had been working on a few things with them during the week, and it left the team feeling pretty confident about their chances.

There had been a lot of emails flying around since Val's preview because there was so much excitement surrounding the upcoming game, so Megs took the opportunity to join in the fray.

The light-hearted banter was then taken to a new level when Val joined the party, signalled by her now famous 'Get This' headline. This one went out to all the Vootball Kids.

GET THIS...

This football game you play is full of weird stuff. And the more I get into the game, the more I find this stuff funny!

- In 2002, a game between Sheffield United and West Bromich Albion (what a cool name!) was abandoned after 82 minutes because there weren't enough players left on the pitch! Sheffield had three sent off and two taken off injured, and were down to 6 men! They were losing 3-0, so the ref stopped the game and left the score at 3-0.

- In 1915, a Middlesbrough vs Oldham match was abandoned after 55 mins when an Oldham player refused to leave the pitch after being sent off. He was then suspended for 12 mths.

- A league game way back in 1895 was abandoned

after 2 mins when a gale-force wind blew the goalposts over. Imagine that!

- Nottingham Forest was the first club to introduce shin pads, nets, the goalpost crossbars and the referee's whistle. Not sure exactly when, but it was in the 1800s. Imagine goals without a crossbar or nets!

- The first live television broadcast was way back in 1938 in the FA Cup Final when Preston beat Huddersfield 1-0.

- In 1985, Danish midfielder Soren Lerby played for Denmark in Ireland, but left the field on 58 minutes when they were leading 3-1 so that he could take a private jet to Germany to play for his club (Bayern Munich). He came on as a half-time sub in a 1-1 draw. He must've slept well that night, huh?

- Only 13 teams entered the first World Cup in Uruguay. Only four non-South American teams (France, Belgium, Yugoslavia + Romania) made the long trip. Now, over 100 countries compete to be one of the 32 teams in the finals. It's the biggest sporting competition in the world.

- Arsenal was the first club in London to turn professional, and is the club with the longest uninterrupted time in the top division. Since 1919, no less. They were formed in 1886.

- Manchester United used to be called Newton Heath, and the players wore yellow and green shirts. The club was formed in 1878 in the Newton Heath suburb of Manchester by workers at the local railway yards. They changed names in 1902 and re-formed as

Manchester United.

- Did you know that the clock out the front of the Man U offices always remains on 3.40pm? Why? It's the time of the plane disaster in 1958 that killed the majority of the players coming back from a European match in Germany.
- After the 1990 World Cup Final in Rome, chunks of the turf from the stadium were sold off... and the net alone earned $5.8 million!! (West Germany won against Argentina, by the way.)
- Alfredo Di Stefano of Real Madrid (same as when Puskas was there) got a half-tonne sculpture of a football made in his back yard. Written on the sculpture was the simple phrase, 'Thanks, old girl.'

Megs replied to Val, messaging via Skype:
I swear you make up some of these things, but even if you do – keep doing it, it's fun!

Val's reply came quickly. She always had Skype open:
I don't make them up. They're true. Cool huh?

Megs's reply was almost as quick: True but weird.

Yeah. I reckon it's because so many people play the game. Means there's more chance of weird things happening. Man, she was a fast typist.

Maybe you're right. Hey, while we're talking weird, here's one for you. I was thinking the other day, do you know what colour hair Abda has? You're her friend and all, and I just wondered. I don't even really know why she wears the headscarf, either, except that it's for religion. I saw an article in the paper the other day saying a girl wearing a headscarf in Canada wasn't allowed to play because of the headscarf, and it just got me thinking, that's all. Does she ever take it off?

Val's answer came promptly:
Hmmm. Never actually seen her hair. Black I guess. We never talk about it.

By then, Megs had been sitting for too long. His feet were itching to move, so he switched off the computer, grabbed the ball from the corner of his room, and went out for a kick. There was just over twenty-four hours before the game against Southside, and he wanted his skills to be razor-sharp.

He practised volleys against the side wall of the house, using the inside of his foot to return the ball to the wall on the full. Where he could, he repeated the skill over and over without having to control the ball with his thigh or chest first, but as long as he kept it in the air, he was happy. His record for repeated first-time volleys crept to twenty-three, but he'd only used his right foot the whole time. *Lazy, Megs, lazy. Use both feet and you'll cause twice the trouble,* Mr Mac would've said if Megs was back in Liverpool.

Next thing he knew, Paloma was zipping towards him, making a bizarre noise Megs guessed (or hoped!) was a truck horn. Her right arm pumped up and down as if pulling on something, and he assumed she was pulling on an imaginary cord that sounded the horn. Either way, Megs was concerned for her sanity – she looked ridiculous!

'What the hell are you doing?' A mixture of shock and dismay showed on his face.

Paloma reached a puffing halt beside him. 'It's my new celebration. What d'ya think?'

'I've seen better – and that's being polite. I'm guessing you're s'posed to be some kind of truck? What's that got to do with anything?'

'Dunno really. Saw a guy from a Spanish Second Division side do it, and I thought it was pretty cool. No?' She seemed less confident.

'I saw a team once who all lined up like ten-pin-bowling pins, then the goal scorer pretended to bowl them all over. They all fell down when the imaginary ball came.' Megs was skilfully avoiding having to answer Paloma. 'And I saw another where the scorer pretended to throw a hand-grenade and all his team-mates fell down around him. Though that probably isn't the best thing to do in this age of terrorism and all that.'

'Yeah, and Archie Thompson and Tim Cahill run to the corner flag and pretend to have a little fight with it. That's pretty funny.' Paloma had taken the hint and moved on as well.

'A cool one is when a guy scores, then goes down to do this to the crowd...' Megs went down on one knee, placed his elbow across that knee as if posing for a photo, then plastered a smug smile onto his face.

'But I can't help it,' he continued as he got back on his feet. 'Even if I plan to do something else, I always run off doing the same thing before I even realise...'

'That's definitely true,' Paloma agreed as she zigzagged around the Morrison front yard with both arms spread wide as if she was a plane in the sky. 'You can always count on the same old Megs celebration!' She was right. Even at training, Megs always did the same thing.

'Ha-ha. I like the shoe-shine as well. That's cool. Or when the team all do a cradle in their arms if one of the team has just had a baby. I think the Brazilians started that a few World Cups ago.' Megs was thinking back to where he'd first seen that one.

'Mark Bresciano's is cool too,' Paloma went on. 'He just stands there like a marble statue and lets everyone run to him. You should've seen it during the Uruguay game to qualify for the World Cup.' She struck a pose just like the Socceroo midfield star, and Megs ran around her in his aeroplane celebration. 'Now that's a cool one,' he yelled as he ran. '*That's* the one you should do rather than pretending to be a truck!'

Paloma thought of another one as Megs continued flying. 'I saw one on YouTube from a few years ago where all the Middlesbrough players ran around flapping their arms like they were geese…'

'Ahhh – I know it,' Megs answered immediately. 'I was still back home then. Apparently they'd had a motivational speech at training where the guy told them they needed to be more like a team – like how birds fly in a big V, and take it in turns to be the leader. The players all thought it was a bit silly, so they made a celebration out of it! It made the papers, but that's what it's like back home. Everything about the game is in the papers.'

'Hmmm. Wonder how long it'll be before you think of here as home, and not England.' Paloma was thinking out aloud.

Megs stopped running. 'That's come up a lot lately, and you know what – I reckon I discovered the answer this morning. When I was speaking to a friend in England, I realised. I reckon I've got two homes – one here and one over there. That way, I don't have to choose.' Megs smiled, then shot off again as if he'd netted the goal that had won Pennendale Wanderers the Champions League.

Nine | All Square at Halfway Mark

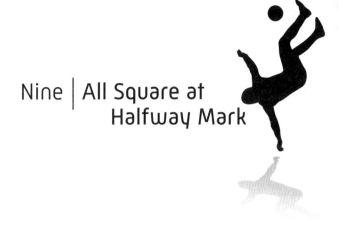

LAST GASP WINNER SECURES
POINTS FOR PENNENDALE

Pennendale Wanderers drew level with Southside Sharks at the top of the Western Region ladder after a hard-fought 2–1 victory claimed maximum points for the away team.

The game was fast-paced and furious, and became increasingly tense as time ticked away. Southside opened the scoring after only 7 minutes when a high, lobbed cross was misjudged by Max in the Pennendale goal. He succeeded in only palming the ball straight to the giant Sharks striker, who lashed the ball home from close range before cruelly taunting the unfortunate keeper by patting the top of his head.

That unsportsmanlike act served to fire the game into overdrive, and high drama was to follow. Southside were repeatedly frustrated by the success of the offside trap Pennendale were playing, and on numerous occasions were asked by the referee to come back when they thought they were through goal. Wanderers' super-coach Atti Czibar had asked his team to adopt this tactic because Southside liked to get the ball forward as quickly as possible. Atti's defenders were asked to push up as close to the halfway line as they could and deny Southside any room. Matteo, in particular, had to be alert to marshall his defensive troopes using this risky system, but he (and they) succeeded admirably.

Defensive troopes… deny them room… offside trap… Megs noted as he continued to scroll down the page. *Val's a natural!*

It wasn't until early in the second half that the score was levelled after Jed 'the Simpfenator' scored a magnificent goal with a low drive from the edge of the box, leaving the Sharks' keeper with no hope. His celebration raised the levels of tension even further after he ran past the Southside supporters with his finger to his lips as if to say 'Shhhhhh…'. It did not, of course, have the desired effect, and the noise around the ground reached new, and unfortunately crass levels.

Megs had to look up 'crass' on dictionary.com, but what Val was saying was absolutely spot on. Some of the language coming from the Sharks' parents was fit for a late night movie on SBS! His heart beat faster as he remembered the sheer excitement of it all.

The game went from end to end, but the real controversy was still to come. With four minutes to go, Megs Morrison won the ball back in a brave tackle in midfield, then set his Pennendale team onto the attack.

Megs Morrison won the ball back in a brave tackle...
Megs couldn't resist rereading that bit.

In one swift movement, Pennendale piled forward, and Paloma threaded a precise through-ball to the onrushing and ever-more-impressive Abda. Her first touch took her into the opposition penalty box, gliding past one of the athletic Southside defenders. Then, just as she was about to shoot, she was tugged back and fell to the ground as if she'd hit a clothesline. It was an obvious penalty, but the Southside supporters still howled their disgust after the referee pointed to the penalty spot.

The dishonourable nature of the act was enhanced by the fact that the defender had pulled Adba back by her flowing headscarf, leaving her black hair exposed. Helped by her team-mates, she immediately did her best to replace the scarf, before Atti substituted her for Sam to finish out the match.

The responsibility of the penalty was accepted by Jed, who was given all manner of abuse by the home supporters as they tried to put him off. But the Simpfenator was made of sterner stuff, and he placed his kick firmly into the bottom left corner to give Pennendale a 2–1 advantage. Once more, he ran to the crowd behind the goal with his finger to his lips before turning to celebrate with his team-mates. The Sharks' players were furious.

Coach Atti tried to remain calm on the sideline, but his

frantic arm gesturing and broken English became more and more difficult to understand as the final minutes ticked by.

We weren't listening by then anyway! Megs thought with a small smile.

In the final twist to the saga, the Sharks had a goal disallowed in the last minute of injury time. As had been a regular occurrence during the match, the Sharks' strikers had strayed into an offside position as the ball was cleared into their direction. The overworked linesman put his flag in the air, but it was initially missed by the referee. On rushed the Southside striker and expertly stuck the ball into the Pennendale net beyond Max. But as he celebrated, the referee was already on his way to speak to the linesman. Offside was given once more, and the team in blue breathed a huge sigh of relief. On the other hand, the team in red and black were incensed and made their feelings known. Almost immediately, the referee blew his whistle to signify the end of the match, then tried to hurry off as quickly as possible as the Southside parents and players crowded around to angrily dispute the outcome.

It was an unsavoury end to a highly tense and exciting affair. This reporter is not the only one who feels that the rivalry born today has not ended with the final whistle of this encounter.

Megs was impressed – excited and impressed. He was excited to think back on the game, and impressed by how brilliantly Val had captured the thrill of it. He decided to email all his teammates and tell them as much.

> Wow!
>
> First, how good is playing competitive football! And second, well done, Val – what a great report.
>
> Three points in the bag and on the same points as those stupid Sharks. I KNEW there was a reason I didn't like Sharks! I don't know about u, but with half the season down and now that we've seen every team, I KNOW we can do it – I just KNOW it.
>
> Megs

It was a conscious choice by Megs not to mention what had happened to Abda, but he did want to know more, so he wrote to Paloma and Val separately.

> Hi Guys,
>
> Is Abda all right? She seemed pretty shaken up. Do you guys know why her headscarf is so important to her?

He was going to remark about now knowing what colour hair she had, but good sense got the better of him, and he kept it to himself. There had been enough controversy in the last couple of days.

For once, it seemed not even Val was online. Megs's question was left unanswered for long enough that Megs started surfing the 'net and lost his earlier train of thought. Who would've thought watching breakdancing on YouTube could be so all consuming!

'You should've seen it! They were going nuts and yelling and having a go at us. It was soooo cool!' Megs was recounting the Sharks game to his dad who had just returned from a week-long trip to Thailand and Vietnam. They were walking down to the park for a kick.

'Yes, I read the report on the internet. That Val certainly is a good writer. Made me feel like I was really there.' Mr Morrison looked at his son. 'So you weren't nervous at the end?'

'Nah, it was cool. Competition does that sort of stuff, and I love it. I wanted it to end because it meant we'd won, but I didn't want it to end, y'know? And you should've seen Jed!' Megs rattled on as fast as a high-speed train. 'I think he loved it more than me. He was baiting the crowd and really turning it on. He made them angry.'

'And how's Abda?' Mr Morrison asked, changing the topic slightly.

Megs was juggling as he spoke and walked – so often had to scurry off to retrieve the ball. But there was no stopping his mouth. 'She was pretty upset when it happened, but now she seems cool. In the end, she was just happy that she was able to win us the penalty. But it's like this League has gone to a whole new level now. Even Atti is more excited about it.'

'Well, there's still lots to do. You're only halfway. But you're in a good position, aren't you. Pretty exciting... Now, do you want to know how Braithwaites is going; whether we're staying in this country or not?'

Due to the excitement surrounding the Sharks game,

Megs realised he hadn't really thought about those issues for a few days. But now that his dad had brought it up, he was instantly intrigued.

'Yeah. How'd it all go over there?'

'Well, for a start, they used those damn chopsticks all the time. I'll really have to practise if I'm going to spend more time in Asia. They use their chopsticks so fast it's a blur, while I struggled to get anything in my mouth! Apart from that, it was a good experience, though, and I managed to get some promising leads. No sales yet, but some good leads and some good contacts, so it was worth it.' It seemed to Megs as if they still didn't know if they were staying or not.

'But I don't get it. If the company doesn't have any money, how come you get to fly to Vietnam and Thailand?' Megs asked.

'Well, it's a cost of the business. I mean, you have to give it a go. At the end of the day, if you don't put your boots on and turn up to the match, then what chance do you have of winning? Do you see what I mean?' Mr Morrison hoped the football parallel would get through to his son.

'So does that mean we're staying?' Megs cut straight to the chase.

'Well, for the time being it does. But nothing has been decided yet. How's your mum? Was she OK in the week?' Mr Morrison changed the subject again.

'She was, actually. Chirpy, in comparison to before. Still a bit weird, but pretty good. At least she wasn't sleeping all the time – although I was getting used to not having to do my teeth and put my dishes away every morning. She's talked heaps about getting a dog. She wants one of those little annoying things though, so we might have to team up over that. I want one of those black-and-white border collies, but Mum reckons they need too much exercise and that I won't do it. Would be a good training partner, I reckon.'

'Is Anfield going to stick?' Mr Morrison asked.

'Think so. No other names have been mentioned.'

By then, they'd reached the park. 'Right then,' said Megs's dad with a clap of his hands. 'What's this sombrero I've heard about?'

Megs began teaching his old man the sombrero. It was much harder to do it on a person so much taller than he was, but Megs still managed it a couple of times. His dad found it much easier over his shorter son.

'You know,' Mr Morrison paused between passes. 'I saw some guys on telly over in Thailand, playing some sort of game with their feet and a cane ball. Keeping it up and playing a kind of volleyball. Just amazing, they were. I think it was called *Takraw*. You might want to YouTube it or something. It could teach you a thing or two…'

Mr Morrison knocked a long, arcing pass towards his son. 'Listen, Megs,' he went on. 'You know that going to England is expensive, and we'll need to have a good think about how to get some money if you win the League. Winning won't mean you can automatically go.'

Megs had already brought the ball under control with the outside of his right foot, and shaped to strike it back where it came. He did so with accurate venom, then awaited his dad's control.

Mr Morrison used his thigh to drop the ball in front of him, then held it still by resting his left foot on top of it. 'Did you hear me, Megs? We don't want you getting too excited just yet. We need you to be realistic about all this.'

'Look, Dad, we're only halfway through the League, I know that. But we'll win it. We have to. We want it more than the other teams. No-one has even talked about how much it'll cost to go, but there'll be a way, surely.'

'I know you don't want to think about it, but you'll have to start thinking soon. Maybe not right now, but if you keep winning... maybe you should quietly speak to Atti about it and see what he thinks. We may have to think of fundraising sooner rather than later. But it'd be a good problem to have, wouldn't it?' Mr Morrison was trying to end on a positive. He always did.

Megs heaved a sigh. 'Yeah, but for now, I just wanna concentrate on playing Bayside again. It's the team I scored a hat-trick against in the first round, so they'll be ready for me this time.'

When the Morrison men arrived home, Mrs Morrison was smiling and waving the local paper around.

'Trying to swat some flies?' Mr Morrison grinned.

'Very funny. Here, something you might want to see

in here.' She handed the *Pennendale Press* to her son.

Megs read aloud: 'Time to Fix the Streets: A Local Survey. The Pennendale Press has conducted an in-depth survey of local residents to deter –'

'No, not that!' his Mum interjected.

Megs picked another headline: 'Are You Getting What You Paid For? There have been increased reports of shop –'

'Since when do you read the front of the newspapers?' interrupted his mum once more. 'Turn to the back.'

And there it was. Megs read aloud with increasing enthusiasm and volume:

TRIP OF A LIFETIME

The winners of this year's Western Region Primary Schools Soccer Competition will jet off to England to tour some of the game's greatest stadiums and play some matches against local competition. And at the halfway mark of the season, our own Pennendale Wanderers are right in the running in their very first season in the League.'

Megs sat down and continued to read. The article gave details of the trip that he and his team-mates had been excited about for weeks, and it made the whole thing seem so much more real. He'd never read so fast, and had to go back over the article a number of times to make sure he hadn't missed anything.

Too excited to sit still, he asked his mum if he could

go and see Paloma, then raced off with the newspaper under one arm, and his football under the other. Arriving on the Mendez doorstep, he asked for Paloma.

'I see you've read the article.' Mrs Mendez pointed to the roll under his arm. 'Paloma hasn't shut up about it! Come in, come in.'

'Thanks. Actually, I might just wait out here.' Megs sprang back restlessly into the Mendez front yard and began to juggle as he waited for Paloma.

Atti had tested out his team at training that week by seeing who could juggle the ball with first-time kicks that went above the juggler's head every time. It was really tough – you had to keep your eye on the ball and be quick on your feet. Megs could only get four the first time he tried. 'It your homework, Wanderers. You have school homework, and you have vootball homework. Everyone to practise and we see who improve.' Atti's words had been echoing in Megs's head since training; his record was now up to eleven.

Paloma bounded into the front yard and distracted Megs with a loud whistle just as he had reached nine. The ball bounced away. 'Paloma! Why'd you do that? I only got nine!' Megs cried in frustration.

'Can't handle the pressure, huh!' Paloma knew how to wind Megs up. 'You'll need to fix that if we want to win this trip! Did you see the article?'

'Sure did. How cool is it! All those stadiums and training facilities. I can't believe it!'

'And games all over the place, too,' Paloma joined in.

'It didn't say how many Premier League games we get

to see, though.'

'No, but there's bound to be some. Will you spend some extra time in Liverpool?' Paloma inquired.

'Dunno. S'pose I will. Maybe we'll stay behind after the official tour. What I'd really like is to play against my old team, the other Wanderers. How weird'd that be!'

Paloma jogged to get the ball (which had rolled to rest under a spiky tree), then back-heeled it to Megs. 'I wonder if Atti would go to Hungary after the tour,' she thought aloud. 'I mean, England isn't far from the rest of Europe; maybe he'd take the chance to go back.'

'Hmmn. Good question. He hasn't been there for fifty years, though. Might be a bit full on… anyway, we aren't there yet,' Megs concluded as he turned on the ball and dribbled away from Paloma. Within a few steps, he'd turned and passed it back to his friend, before running even wider on the front lawn. 'Come on then, cross it over here. On my head!'

Paloma knew the drill, and clipped the ball first time in front of Megs's running path. It was a perfectly weighted pass, and Megs launched himself at the ball at full stretch – kind of like Superman but without the cape and without the red underwear on the outside of his shorts. He connected with a thud, and the ball flew off towards the side of the Mendez house, narrowly missing the lounge room window, but landing right between the two trees that made up the goal.

Megs sprang back up from the ground, and charged off with arms spread and mouth open wide. 'Ye-esss!'

'I thought you were going to try another celebration

– you know, do something new,' Paloma laughed.

'Yeah, well, I can never remember to do them when I get excited, so I'm over it; I'm just gonna stick with whatever happens,' came the puffed-out reply.

The two Pennendale Wanderers continued to kick the ball around the Mendez front yard until the sun started to drop. Paloma was getting better and better at the sombrero, but Megs was not so slick at it. Paloma was knocking in some great crosses for Megs to practise all sorts of headers and acrobatic overhead kicks, but she wasn't interested when Megs returned the favour. She was great at volleys, but not interested in scissor kicks or headers – and especially not diving headers.

'But it's a part of the game, Paloma,' Megs would cry out every time Paloma chickened away from a header. 'You look like a turtle when you pull your neck in like that!'

'Yeah, well, at least I won't get into trouble from my mum. Look at the grass stains you have all over you from diving all over the place.' It was the only comeback Paloma seemed able to come up with.

As it grew darker, they sat and read the newspaper article again – spending time on the player profiles that Val had sent to the paper a few weeks earlier, without telling anyone at school. After the introductory paragraph, the paper went on to talk about the implications of the trip for kids' football in general.

Western Region Primary Schools' Board member Simon Prior was the driving force behind the trip, and as an ex-professional player in the north of England, was the one with all the contacts. *'Look, football is just booming in this country, and now's the time for people like me to help fuel that interest,'* says Mr Prior. *'It's like some kind of revolution. All the kids love the EPL [English Premier League], so what better way to fire them up than to offer a prize that lets them see it, lets them play against kids their own age, and gives them a glimpse of what football is like over there?'*

There are ten teams in this year's competition, and if incentives like this continue annually, the Board will certainly have some organising to do. Mr Prior continued, *'We could've had fourteen teams this year, but couldn't include them all. Next year we'll probably have over twenty, so we'll have to run two competitions in parallel, then have a playoff to get the overall winner. On top of that, from what I've seen of this year's competition, the standard has really improved, and the teams are obviously training hard and really developing. That's the benefit of the trip from our point of view. The whole League is improving already.'*

The details of the trip are being finalised, but the Pennendale Press can confirm the following:

Manchester United

> - tour plus training facilities and game vs United U/12

Manchester City

> - tour

Liverpool

> – tour plus training facilities and game vs Liverpool U/12

Middlesbrough

> - tour plus training facilities

Arsenal

> - tour

West Ham

> - tour plus training facilities

Coventry City

> - game vs under-13s

Exeter

> - game vs under-13s.

Each leg will include historical and cultural aspects as well as football insights, and of course there will be top-level games to watch from the stands.

Mr Prior is a passionate driver of this competition, and had more to add. *'It's important not only to see the biggest and the best like Man United and Liverpool, but also some of the lower leagues like Coventry and*

Exeter. The game is not just about the top of the top, even though that's where we all want to be. I still do now!'

Mr Prior will lead the tour group, and admits that while subsidised, the trip will not be free. *'We are doing what we can to get sponsors and keep the costs down as much as possible, but there will have to be some fundraising. There are three months between the end of the season here and the projected departure date, so hopefully that will give enough time [to organise fundraising].'*

At the halfway mark, our own Pennendale Primary Wanderers are well in contention, especially after scoring an emotional and exciting win last week against the team tipped as competition favourites, the Southside Sharks.

Coach Atti Czibar is an ex-professional from Hungary, but hadn't been involved in the game for fifty years since coming to Australia. *'These players make me not want to miss vootball any more,'* said an emotional Czibar. *'They get me involved again and I love them for it. These are my Vootball Kids and I very proud. First year in competition, and we are in good position. Let's see what happens from here.'*

Budding journalist and Pennendale student Val Teresi has compiled the following profiles of the Pennendale Wanderers squad:

ATTI – **COACH:** school cleaner and ex-international player with Hungary. Quiet on the sidelines unless it's tense, when his face contorts and his arms start waving all over the place. Age: unknown.

MAX – **GOALKEEPER:** 'Maxy' is big and brave with massive hands. Wanted to be a better outfield player, but was too good in goals and now loves it there. Age: 12.

MATTEO – **DEFENDER:** graceful and elegant and always seems to have time on the ball. Quiet, but leads by example and rarely makes mistakes. Age: 11.

SEB – **DEFENDER:** 'Sebulous' is big and strong with aspirations of being a rock star. Sometimes gets caught in possession, but makes up for it with his love of tackling. Age: 11.

ANGELIQUE – **DEFENCE:** 'Angel' is quick and agile, she provides excellent cover and never seems to get tired. Age: 12.

ADAM – **WIDE DEFENCE OR MIDFIELD:** 'Ads' likes to be tricky on the ball and has a great left foot. Can run and run and run. Age: 12.

DANNY – **WIDE DEFENCE OR MIDFIELD:** Very similar to Adam, but on the right side. Stands out with his yellow boots. Age: 12.

IVAN – **MIDFIELD:** 'Ivie' is tall with long legs that help him cover the ground quickly. Doesn't like running much; however, is an excellent passer and has great vision. Age: 11.

ABDA – **MIDFIELD:** A great improver throughout the season. Graceful and athletic and getting trickier and trickier. Plays with a smile but is surprisingly competitive. Age: 12.

EDWARD – **MIDFIELD:** 'Megs' is the engine of the team and like a little terrier when he wants the ball. Loads of tricks and great skill, he makes up for his lack of height with his pace and ability. Scores goals, too. Age: 11.

BISCAN – **MIDFIELD/ATTACK:** Still learning English, but a huge asset to the team. Excellent dribbler, but doesn't like to pass much. Likes being out wide and embarrassing defenders. Age: 12.

MITCH – **UTILITY:** Quiet, but keen to learn and getting better all the time. Always follows Atti's directions to the letter. Age: 11.

PALOMA – **ATTACK:** A livewire who always seems to be in the right place at the right time. Fast and enthusiastic, she always causes trouble for opposition defences with her intelligent movement and skill. Age: 11.

JED – **ATTACK:** 'The Simpfenator' is powerful and direct, and full of confidence. Plays best when provoked, and expects a lot from his team-mates. Leading goal scorer at this stage. Age: 12.

By the time Megs and Paloma had finished reading, their eyes were straining in the dusk. Finally it became too difficult, and they decided to call it quits. Megs rolled the paper back under his arm, flicked up the ball and headed home.

As the weeks passed, Pennendale and Southside continued neck-and-neck at the top of the table, with Brenthill Catholic and Hills Rockets making their move to be still in the running. Pennendale had had four wins and a draw since beating the Sharks, and the Sharks had had four wins and a loss (to Brenthill) over the same period.

ROUND 14				
CLUB	W	L	D	Pts
Pennendale Wanderers	**10**	**1**	**3**	**33**
Southside Sharks	10	2	2	32
Hills Rockets	8	2	4	28
Brenthill Catholic	8	2	4	28

Paloma had hit a rich vein of scoring to overtake Jed as the Wanderers' top scorer, with Megs in third place with a great return from midfield. Crowds were starting to get bigger, and interest around the playground was definitely growing. Big Mr Jackson, the school Principal, had even been spotted at the last couple of games.

But it wasn't just on the League ladder that the Wanderers/Sharks rivalry was intensifying. Things were turning nasty off the pitch as well.

Ten | 'Headscarf Horror Sets Ugly Standard'

'Have you seen what they're saying? Who do they think they are?'

'What are you nattering about?' Megs heard Paloma's angry question as he joined her, Matteo and Adam before training.

'What the Sharks are saying on the forums,' Adam replied.

'Guess they're just trying to put us off,' suggested Matteo.

'I reckon. 'Specially since we've already beaten them once.'

'Well, they'll have to do better than that. Pretty gutless though.'

Megs still looked mystified. Paloma turned to him. 'Haven't you seen the chats?'

'Nah. Been too busy with Mum and Dad. They've got a new lease on life lately, and want to do stuff all the time when Dad's around. Sightseeing, board games, walks. It's full-on,' Megs sounded weary.

'Have a look when you get home tonight. They've

been ripping into the lot of us. Even Atti, but especially Jed. Pretty cruel to Abda, as well.'

'How's their form?' added Ivan as he joined the group with Danny and Biscan. 'Where do they get off?'

'I know. We were just talking about it,' Adam replied.

Ivan continued, 'The best bit was when that guy wrote: "They're soft and weak and, without crazy referee decisions, we'd have smashed them." What a load of –'

'– I know,' Paloma cut in. 'But when they started having a go at Abda, that's when it got me. Hope she hasn't read it.'

Just then, that very person joined the group. Smiling and perky, she seemed the opposite of upset. Paloma was relieved that Abda obviously hadn't seen what was written about her and her 'stupid scarf'.

But Abda surprised them, 'So you've all seen the forums. I'm guessing that's what you're talking about. How FUNNY are they! We obviously have them rattled. We played them weeks ago, and they're still going on about it. What losers. And when that guy wrote: "Beware of Trengal this week, you're in for a surprise," what was he trying to do? Scare us? They'll have to do better than that!'

'Hey Abda,' Ivan ran his fingers through his hair as he spoke. 'Why *do* you wear that headscarf?'

'Iv-eee…' Paloma scolded, showing how uneasy she felt for Abda. Some of the other kids immediately looked at the ground, sharing Paloma's discomfort. But all of them wanted to know the answer.

'No, no, that's cool. It's no biggie,' Abda smiled.

'You don't have to…' Paloma continued.

'Look, it's easy.' Abda was happy to explain. 'The scarf is a sign of modesty and pride in being a Muslim. I don't have to wear it, but I want to out of respect for my religion. I decided I would about two years ago when I came to Pennendale. Some women wear the full face-covering hijab, but that's not for me.'

'So, what, it's like a Jewish kid wearing one of those caps, or me wearing one of these crosses round my neck?' Adam pulled a gold chain from inside his shirt.

'Pretty much, I s'pose,' Abda agreed.

'A bit more obvious though,' Megs said from the group.

'No more obvious than you wearing a Liverpool shirt instead of an Everton one!' Abda was enjoying herself. 'And the choice to wear it means a lot.'

'How many gods do you have?' Adam was getting into this. All the Kids in the group waited curiously; they were glad Adam asked.

'Well, for us there's only one God,' Abda replied. 'It's the same one that Christians and Jews believe in as well.'

'Really?' Ivan was surprised.

'Then how come you wear a scarf and I wear a cross?' Adam was firing on all cylinders.

'Dunno, really. I 'spose that's just your choice about what you believe,' Abda replied.

'How do you keep it on when you run around?'

Danny asked.

'I wear one with elastic, but you can do them with pins, too.' Abda showed the elasticated part as she spoke.

'You people! You little people standing talking over there!'

It was Atti, limping towards them with the bag of balls slung so far over one shoulder that they dragged on the ground. 'You always stand around and talk. You do that later. Here, you make the balls do the talk,' and he tipped out the balls onto the dusty ground. 'One ball each and you juggle. Warm-up juggle like normal, then I want see who has done homework. Who is better at juggle each touch from foot above the head. *Ugyan!*'

The Vootball Kids had assumed over the last couple of months that Ugyan meant 'Now' or 'Go' in Hungarian, so they immediately grabbed a ball each. As they started juggling, they soon forgot what they had been deep in discussion about earlier. When you're concentrating properly on the ball, Megs thought, everything else clears out of your head.

'Stop. All stop.' Atti glanced towards Jed and Max, ambling down towards the training session, then, turning towards the team, he whispered, 'When they get close, I want all you to clap and cheer...'

'Welcome boys! You take your time. Whenever you ready, you join us,' called Atti sarcastically as the Wanderers obediently clapped and cheered. 'You take your time, huh. Right – you know what happens if late. Down, and give me fifteen!' The team got the impression Atti actually liked it when people were late to training.

Those who were late didn't, though, so it didn't happen too often.

'OK, time to show me homework,' Atti continued once they'd all counted out fifteen push-ups for the unfortunate Simpfenator and Max.

Most of the team had obviously done their homework, because everyone was better than the week before. Megs managed to get his record up to seventeen, even using his left foot on two occasions. The next best was Biscan with fifteen, then Matteo with eleven. Max was the worst with two.

The rest of the session was fairly lightweight and skills based, because the game against the Trengal Tigers had been brought forward to the following day and Atti wanted his players fresh. They played head tennis, tried to keep the ball up in small groups, then did some shooting practice. The aim was to hit the ball right into the corners without belting it. 'Must place ball so keeper have no chance. Relax in front of goal. Goal is big, ball is small. To score is easy,' Atti would repeat over and over.

By the time Megs got home, finished his dinner (how he loved shepherd's pie) and did some homework, he was exhausted. He took five minutes to read the forums everyone had been talking about at training – they really were pretty fierce – then went to bed. There was a game against Trengal the next day, and rest was vital.

'Sorry, but I just can't allow it,' the referee repeated.

'It's never been problem before!' Atti argued, growing ever more frustrated with the referee.

'Come on, what does it matter? Do you know what you're doing?' asked the tall, blond, muscular man who was evidently the Tigers' coach.

'Well, it's in the rules, and we've been told to look out for it. If she takes it off, she can play, otherwise she can't play at all.' The referee had been speaking with both coaches for the last five minutes. By this stage though, the players had begun crowding around the referee and their coaches, sensing something was up.

'Well, you tell them, Mr Referee, because I not going to!' Atti was fuming.

'What's going on?' Max asked on behalf of the Wanderers.

The referee looked nervous. 'I'm sorry, but I cannot allow anyone wearing a headscarf to play. Just as no-one can wear jewellery, you can't wear a headscarf.'

Everyone whipped their heads around to look at Abda, who blushed red, looking like she wanted to become invisible.

'But that's... when... it's never been an issue before!' Paloma finally got it out.

'Sorry, but they're the rules.'

'Come on, ref – what harm can it do?' This time it was one of the Tigers' players. 'It's not like it's the wrong colour or anything!' He was right; Abda always wore a blue headscarf on match days.

By now, Angelique had her arm around Abda who had begun to tremble under all the unwanted attention.

'Look, kick-off is in one minute. I'm sorry, but it can either be removed, or anyone wearing a headscarf can't play.' The referee was doing his best not to speak directly to Abda, but he might as well have been right up in her face.

Abda began to get teary, as more of her team-mates and Atti crowded around her to provide some consolation.

'Abda?' Atti led her away from the crowd. 'What do you want to do?'

She sniffed and wiped away some tears. 'I won't play. I won't take it off and we have to win, so I won't play. You don't need me, and we need three points.'

'Need you or not need is not the point. You should not have to do anything you not want to.' Atti beckoned Val over from the sideline to comfort Abda, then called his team in close.

'You heard referee. He make a stupid call, but he is the referee.' Atti's hands were shaking, his bright eyes shinier than usual. 'Abda say she won't play so we still can. It wrong she have to make that decision, but that is what she said.'

Megs was feeling decidedly uncomfortable. His cheeks were hot and he couldn't stand still. He desperately wanted get those points – but this wasn't right.

The ref blew his whistle. The game had to get underway, and the Tigers were already in position. They had confused looks on their faces, but they were ready to go.

None of the Wanderers moved from their huddle, as Val hugged the teary Abda, now at the side of the pitch.

The ref blew again – this time with extra urgency.

Parents and friends on the sidelines were puzzled. Only the little section of Sharks players that had come along to watch seemed happy, perhaps sensing their greatest rivals might be thrown off their game.

By now Megs's stomach churned, as though something was burning in there right up to his chest.

Then Jed spoke up from the back of the pack, and broke the spell. His voice was strong and clear. 'This isn't right. I'm trying to figure it out, but it doesn't seem fair. What happens if we don't play?'

'We don't play, we lose the game,' Atti replied.

'Well, I can't play feeling like this. Don't know about you lot.' Jed spoke clearly as he looked around his huddled team-mates.

Megs knew what he meant, so he piped up too. 'I agree. Stuff it.'

Immediately the words came out of his mouth, the burning in his stomach stopped. There was much nodding and murmured agreement among the Wanderers.

The whistle sounded once more. 'Last chance, Pennendale!' called the referee.

Atti surveyed his charges, then turned to the referee.

'I think we not play. Bye bye.' He walked over to Adba and Val, followed closely by his team.

The referee stood, stunned. This was something he had not expected. And what happened next added to his surprise.

The Trengal Tigers left the field, too. They walked over to Pennendale, with comments like, 'Look what you've done,' and 'There's no need,' as they passed the referee.

The big blond coach approached the referee and said pointedly, 'This is not us accepting a forfeit. This is us forfeiting, too. You will hear more about this!' He spoke clearly and loudly to make sure the crowd could hear every word.

Adba didn't know whether to laugh or cry, so she did both.

Together, both teams left the ground, voicing their disgust but connected by the whole unfortunate situation.

The referee remained a lonely figure in the middle of the pitch, his whistle in his hand, but with no-one left to blow it for.

The next day, Val's match report could only address one issue, since there was no game to report on. So address it she did, recounting the events in vivid colour and with strong emotion.

The report was placed on the internet as well as emailed around, and by the end of the weekend it had created the biggest fuss of all the reports that season. Emails, messaging, phone calls and texts began flying around the Pennendale area as a result of the controversy. Before long, the Wanderers' new friends at Trengal had joined in. There was confusion, anger, misunderstanding and even the odd bad joke.

Megs passed on the news he'd read a couple of weeks ago about the young Muslim girl in Canada, and some other people remembered a couple of years ago something similar happening with a girl playing for an all-girls' team in Melbourne. Both teams had walked off then, as well.

The controversy continued for the next few days, getting further inflamed when the *Pennendale Press* ran with the story on the Wednesday morning, using Val's report and adding their own take. The headline 'Headscarf Horror Sets Ugly Standard' set the tone for the article. Val was horrified to see how her match report was being used, but to the newspaper it was gold-dust.

Within hours, national television stations and newspapers were on the case, and talkback radio was jam-packed with callers wanting to discuss the issue. Even some international media were jumping on board.

By Wednesday night, the news became less and less about the incident itself, and more and more about bigger issues of religion, racism, bullying, Australia's freedoms, and even about terrorism.

It was big stuff, and it was important stuff, but naturally the Vootball Kids', main cause of upset was about the way Abda had been treated – not all the stuff the newspapers were writing about. They wondered about the rules and whether Abda would be allowed to play again, but they didn't expect to have to face questions about all the 'bigger picture' issues the media were so intent on discussing.

It was one thing giving 'TV responses' to Val's interviews before games, but Megs found having actual TV cameras shoved in his face outside the schoolgrounds something different altogether. The fun of it was gone, and all he could do was blink into the bright lights and answer, 'Don't know,' to most of the questions. He was in unfamiliar territory.

Abda, on the other hand, was handling the situation calmly and gracefully. Outwardly, she seemed to understand what was going on, and, supported by her parents whenever media was around, she did nothing that might make the situation worse. She said things like, 'I'm sure the referee had his reasons. He seemed a bit upset by it, too,' and 'I'm just sorry I couldn't play, and feel bad that everyone else left the field, too, though I thank them for their understanding every day.' Other than that, it was 'no comment' all-around.

Word had also filtered through that the Western Region Board had made a judgement on the outcome of the abandoned match. Even though Trengal had also chosen to forfeit the game, they had left the field after Pennendale had already forfeited, so would therefore be awarded the win by default. The impact of the news was overwhelming. Trengal – who only had three points to their name by that stage – just picked up another three at the expense of the high-flying Wanderers. That meant that the Southside Sharks moved back into first place, two points ahead of the Pennendale team.

The season was approaching its final stages, and now it was an entirely new ball game.

ROUND 15				
CLUB	W	L	D	Pts
Southside Sharks	**11**	**2**	**2**	**35**
Pennendale Wanderers	10	2	3	33
Hills Rockets	8	2	5	29
Brenthill Catholic	8	3	4	28

Eleven | More Than Meets the Eye

'But why would they say these things? How could they know?' Val hadn't stopped furrowing her brow since the incident with Abda five days ago.

While everyone else was a bit shell-shocked by it all and were following Abda's lead of trying to stay calm, Val had gone into overdrive. She'd asked Paloma and Megs to meet her in the school library before school.

'Do you really think that's true?' Paloma was starting to get a bit agitated, too. 'It does make sense...'

'I'm convinced. Why else would this happen now and not before? There had to be something, and I think this is it.' Val was steely.

Megs was a kick behind the play. 'Explain it to me again. Just so I'm clear.'

At that moment, Atti's bucket and mop came past the library door, followed closely by the old cleaner. He called out, 'Hello, you. Now this is interesting. Val I see in here before, but never with you two – Mr Megs and Miss Paloma. So now I think something is up. You hatching something and I think, Miss Val, you know all about it.

You know the school asked everybody to be calm about this Abda stuff, no? And you know Abda doesn't want a fuss, OK?'

The trio were a bit sheepish, but after spending so much time on the sidelines with Atti over the last few months, Val was getting to know him well. And she knew Atti was as upset about the whole situation as she was. So she took a punt.

'Atti, come in here and have a look at this. I need to explain it again to Megs anyway. His brain doesn't work properly until recess, I reckon.' She smiled, trying to lighten the mood.

'Or when there is vootball in front of him!' Atti teased, entering the room.

'There's no point me coming early, there really isn't!' Megs said crossly. 'All that happens is that everyone makes fun of me!' He continued flatly, 'Just tell us again.'

'OK, here we go. Now I reckon something was a bit suss about the ref not letting Abda play…' Val risked a sideways glance at Atti.

'Va–al…' came the sing-song reply from the old cleaner. 'I knew you were up to something!' There was a pause, then Atti grinned. 'Good girl. I glad. So, *ugyan*, what you think?'

Val, Paloma and Megs all laughed with relief. They weren't in trouble. Atti was on board.

Val continued the story. 'I mean, why has this never happened before? And Abda's right, I reckon the ref was a bit uncomfortable about the whole thing. So I've been racking my brains…'

'You're good at that,' Megs joked, trying to get his own back, but Val ignored him and kept talking.

'... and then I went back over some of the forum entries and emails and all that stuff that the Sharks were saying after we beat them, and I started to think I was onto something.'

'And?' Atti was leaning over them, eager to find out more.

'Well, check this one out.' Paloma leaned forward and read aloud from the forum entry thread titled 'Look Out, Wanderers'. Her voice was low and clear:

Be aware of Trengal next week, u r in for a surprise.

Sometimes winning is playing by the rules.

Not like when you beat us. LOSERS!

Can't wait to play u again. It's us that'll win the Trip.

It's not right u have so many girls – and ONE girl in particular. Sharks RULE!

'So? I think I'm missing something...' Megs spoke for Atti as well as himself. Obviously this stuff wasn't the nicest thing to be reading, but the Sharks were their closest rivals in the Championship, so it was not too unexpected.

'Well, look at the name of the guys who started the thread.' Paloma was onto it.

Thomo was the signature.

'Now look at the email address,' she continued.

They looked at the line of small print:
christhompsonstar12@hotmail.com

Megs and Atti looked at each other blankly.

Val took up the explanation again. 'Chris Thompson is that big striker with the Sharks. Good player, but mean. His dad is a guy called Ken Thompson, and Ken Thompson is involved with soccer at all sorts of levels. He's a powerful guy who is also a big boss at 'Thomo and Tex Real Estate'. Also, he was on the Board of the Western Region soccer right up until last year. I've heard my mum and her friends speak about him before – and it's never particularly nice stuff!'

'Keep talking,' said Megs slowly. He was not much closer to grasping how all this affected Abda and the Wanderers, but he was certainly intrigued, and trying to keep up. This was like some sort of spy movie!

'Well, check out what they're saying.' It was Paloma's turn again. *Get ready for a surprise against Trengal. One girl in particular. Sometimes winning is playing by the rules…'*

'That's the bit that got me thinking.' Val joined in again. 'It's a weird thing to say – especially for the Sharks. *Sometimes winning is playing by the rules.* It's like they all knew something we didn't. *Then,* I also found out that the referee works at Thomo and Tex Real Estate. Look – here's his photo!' Val pointed vigorously at a web page she had opened earlier.

Atti removed his battered cap and ran his knobbly fingers through what was left of his stringy hair. 'I hope you have some more to add to this story…'

'Sure do!' Val was on a roll. 'I couldn't get that "playing by the rules" bit out of my mind, so Pal and I got to talking about it. We looked into the newspaper article Megs had seen about the girl in Canada, and also when it happened in Australia a couple of years ago. That girl was playing for South Melbourne Women's – the club Puskas used to coach. There was nothing to say definitely why those girls with the headscarves couldn't play, apart from how the rules were understood. The referees are there to enforce the rules, they don't make them up. So we looked up the rules.'

'And on top of that, don't you remember the ref saying he'd been told to look out for this?, Paloma asked. 'Look up the rules for them,' she suggested, pointing at the computer.

'Well,' Val spoke as she fiddled around on the internet, 'the Western Region rules just follow the international laws of the game, and they are set by FIFA. Here we are... fifa dot com.'

Val buzzed around the website until she found 'Laws of the Game' and went to Section Four: 'The Players' Equipment'.

'See, look, there is an immediate reference to safety and correct colours.' She pointed to the screen and they all read:

A player must not use equipment or wear anything that is dangerous to himself or another player (including any kind of jewellery).

Val continued. 'Then, later on, the site outlines some recent versions of the rules published by International Football Associations, saying that players' equipment can't have slogans, advertising, political, religious or personal statements. So it's not very clear at all, but if he wanted to, a ref could say the headscarf is dangerous to the player or other players.'

'That's what happened in that Canada example, wasn't it? From memory, there was something about how the headscarf could choke somehow.' Megs was awake now.

'Sure was,' Paloma replied. 'So here's what we think. We reckon the referee was put under some pressure to interpret the rules that same way. We reckon the Sharks – or the Sharks' parents more likely because the Sharks aren't that smart – found out about the laws after that guy pulled Abda back by her scarf and gave away the penalty, and I reckon they made the most of it. And the Sharks' players must've all known what was going to happen as well. It was all planned so they'd put us off!'

'Well, if that's what they did, it sure worked. They also got back above us on the ladder because Trengal got the three points.' Megs was going red in the face.

'No wonder they were in the crowd that day. Thought they looked smug.' Paloma was visibly angry as she thought back on it.

'Hmmm. Unfortunately that story make sense. I guess big competition does that to some people.' Atti was obviously pretty angry about what he'd just been told, but he was trying not to let it get to him. 'But it still not change anything. They still two points ahead of us,' he concluded as he about-faced and limped out of the room.

'Well, if we don't do something, then Abda might never be able to play again,' pleaded Paloma to Atti's back. 'We have to do something.'

'Perhaps, yes.' He didn't turn around, so his voice was difficult to hear. 'But also remember Abda wants the whole thing to stop. She feel bad enough already for losing three points last time, even though it isn't her fault. She might not thank you for doing something.'

Then the bell sounded and the three Vootball Kids had to leave their frustrated discussions and scheming behind. As they left for class, Megs wondered aloud, 'Can you wear a hat when you play? A keeper can, so can outfield players as well? The rules don't say you can't. And what about wearing glasses? I've played against plenty of people wearing glasses – they'd be more dangerous than a hat or headscarf, wouldn't they?'

Atti was at training early the next night, with cones set out and balls strategically placed. As soon as his charges arrived, they were given a ball and a task. Juggling with feet only. Juggling with head only. Or thighs only. For Megs, only the outside of either foot. Others were just to dribble, or practise tricks (including the sombrero). Atti was a firm believer in action being the best remedy for anxiety, and after the recent unpleasantness, he wanted his Vootball Kids to enjoy the game again.

'Right. When I blow whistle, you all stop the ball, then practise new thing. Skill, skill, skill. Vootball is for dancing with your feet and the ball. Dance, dance, dance. Get on your toes and dance with ball!'

After fifteen minutes, he brought everyone in. 'OK,' he said, showing every crooked tooth in his smile. 'We learn lots so far, and you have improved very much this year. And we are in a great position in the competition. But we have had heavy week, and as competition keeps going, it might get heavier. So we play light. We play with smiles. Abda still smiling, then we all keep smiling too. So now… let's practise something different. I noticed not enough silly celebrations when you score. Some, also, are not smart ones… true, Simfenate?' Atti put his fingers to his lips and shushed Jed with a smile. The Vootball Kids (including Jed) chuckled.

'Then there's Mr Megs,' and Atti half ran, half hobbled in circles with his arms outstretched. The chuckles then turned into laughter when Atti made fun of Matteo, 'You defenders not know what to do when you score, but to just stand there, shrugging your shoulders!' Atti then did a great rendition of Matteo's confused expression and up-faced palms after scoring against Penders Grove a couple of weeks ago.

'So I want to see more!' he concluded. Let's have some fun with this game!' Megs surreptitiously looked over to Paloma and cheekily pretended to pull on a truck horn.

'I've got one!' It was Max – the goalkeeper. Everyone laughed.

'Go on then. This'll be good!' Jed piped up.

'No, no, think of it. We're one–all against the Sharks with one minute to go, and we have a corner.' Max was very animated. 'I come up for it because we need to win. The ball gets pumped in, and there are bodies everywhere. But I jump above all of 'em, and get my head to it. BANG – it flies into the top corner and the other keeper doesn't move. Then, I run straight to their goalkeeper and stand next to him on the line and pretend to help him!'

Jed gave Max a massive high-five as everyone laughed. 'Like it, man, that'd show him!'

For the next five minutes, everyone enjoyed making fools of themselves and laughing at the stupid celebrations. There were silly walks, handstands, patting on their own backs and all sorts of crazy antics. Abda even started spinning so fast in her head scarf and gown it looked like she would take off.

Then, it was straight into a game of six on six… where goals didn't count if Atti thought the celebration wasn't good enough.

When the session had finished, all the Kids were much cheerier. Even Val – who was taking notes from the sidelines – had a big smile on her face. Atti called her over to join the group.

'Well done, you Vootball Kids,' said Atti, turning to look at each of the kids as he spoke. 'I very proud of all of you. The school very proud of you and your parents very proud of you. You stick up for each other, and that important everywhere. Not just on vootball pitch, but everywhere. And that is what will win us Championship. I sure of it!

'Now, all the parents have been sneaky and we all talk,' he continued, 'and guess what? This Saturday, we going out! We have a bye this week, so we going to see a match on Saturday instead.' Atti was smiling his crooked smile, as the Vootball Kids looked at each other in surprise, wondering if anyone else knew what was going on. Atti loved this stuff.

'We have got a big batch of tickets for Sydney FC to play Melbourne Victory! We go to game, then we get pizza. What you think?' he finished triumphantly.

What did they think? The Vootball Kids were thrilled, and immediately began running around recreating their goal celebrations once more. Megs was about to watch his first live professional game since leaving England. He was buzzing, even if it wasn't the mighty Reds.

Above the craziness, Atti called out, 'Have a good night – and remember – vootball is light, vootball should not be heavy! Bye bye.' With that, the old man hitched up his bag of balls and limped away through the dust. Those players that stopped their celebrations to look after him could only see the back of his head as he ambled away, but if they could've seen the front, Megs was sure they might have observed a small, satisfied smile spread across their coach's wrinkly face.

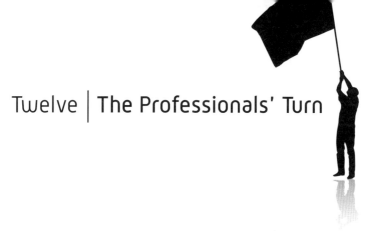

Twelve | The Professionals' Turn

The Vootball Kids left their parents behind as they bounced up the stairs towards the second level. People were swarming around with drinks in hand, and often, food already in their mouths. Most people were dressed in sky-blue, but every now and then, some opposition navy-blue could be seen as well. Among the noise and bustle, there was a feeling of nervous excitement. People moved as if they had somewhere to be.

As soon as the Kids had seen the sloping, high-tech, white roof of the stadium in the distance, the pace had lifted. Seeing where they would spend the next few hours watching top-level football produced a surge of energy. And now that they were actually inside the Sydney Football Stadium, they could barely contain their excitement.

Megs had been to live football games before. Most of them were at Liverpool's famous Anfield ground, and he'd even been to the home of his great rivals in blue – Everton. For a treat one time, his uncle had taken him to see Manchester United play at Old Trafford, and then there was the time on their family holiday to Switzerland where he and his dad watched a game while Mrs Morrison shopped. Some 'me time', as both his parents called it. The pitch that day was perfect – even in the freezing winter – and Megs was disappointed to realise (only after a full thirty minutes of watching the game!) that the grass was actually fake. But no matter which stadium, or which game, Megs always felt the same excitement. This time, it was for Sydney FC vs Melbourne Victory, and his heart was pounding as if it were a World Cup Final.

As the Kids got to their level and saw the numbered sign pointing to their seats, Megs slowed right down. The others were already bounding through the door and into the sunlight, but Megs held back a little. He turned to see the group of chattering parents coming up the stairs behind him (thankfully his dad wasn't one of those wearing a crazy, blue-haired, spiky wig), then looked down at the precious ticket he held firmly in his hand.

More slowly now, he made his way towards the entrance to the arena. He didn't like to rush this bit, because it could only be done once per game, and it always took his breath away.

Soon, Megs could hear the growing buzz of the crowd. He was buffeted a few times by hastier fans as he walked, but he barely noticed. The ground announcer began calling out the team names, each one followed by cheers from fans.

Megs made his way up the last little flight of stairs, his heart pounding. All he could see now were the stairs in front of him, and the sky above – as blue as the Sydney

FC colours. With every step up, Megs felt his heart beat faster.

Left foot, right foot. The crowd noise grew louder. The sun got brighter. One more step and he'd be there.

He could almost feel the crowd's excitement in his blood, although he still couldn't see the ground.

Left foot – and there it was. Sky-blue dotted all the way down the stadium seating, and people everywhere. Flags were swinging and banners were draped over the edges of the stands. Megs's senses quickly took it all in, until his eyes rested on the playing surface. It was the greenest of green, the flattest of flat. But oddly, it was the white he saw first – the precise sidelines and centre circle. The eighteen-yard box and the penalty spot. The crisp goalposts and box-styled nets that looked like they'd never been used before.

A mixture of envy and anticipation came over him as he saw the players going through their final warm-up. To most people, the scene was a fantasy world – one to watch, enjoy and discuss. But Megs saw it differently. He knew they were real people down there warming up. He knew it was real grass, real white lines and a real ball. The rules down there were exactly the same as the rules of the game he played, and the ball was just as round. One day, Megs was sure he'd be one of those people down on the pitch. One day, other people would walk up stadium stairs full of excitement to watch him play.

'Can I help you find your seat?' It was a teenager with a fluorescent yellow vest and a face full of pimples.

Megs showed him his ticket, but before the usher

could direct him, the Vootball Kids called to him. 'Megs! Over here! Come on – what kept you?'

Megs walked along the empty row behind all the Kids, then jumped over into his seat between Matteo and Adam. Before long, all the parents came along and filled up the empty seats behind them. As soon as they sat down, Max's dad called out, 'Righto! Who wants a hot dog?' Of course they all did, but no-one wanted to leave their seat and risk missing the start of the match. Before anyone could point this out, Max's dad spoke up again. 'Don't worry, you don't have to get up...' He reached into his bag, and pulled out a plastic bag full of long white rolls. He passed them to Atti, who was sitting next to him, before going back into his bag and getting a jumbo-sized thermos. Megs wasn't the only one who was puzzled. Everyone stared.

Max's dad smiled as he unscrewed the lid. Steam rose from the top. He then took what looked to be a chopstick out of his pocket, and poked inside the thermos. To cheers, he then pulled out a steaming frankfurt, and placed it inside a roll. 'There we go. Who's up? There's plenty to go around!'

'Genius!' said Mr Morrison, clapping.

'Well, it beats eight dollars each or whatever they're charging here! Sauce anyone?' Max's dad waved the plastic bottle above his head.

By then, the players had left the pitch, and a few groundsmen were busily flattening any areas of the ground that had been roughened during the warm-up. Matteo leaned over to Megs and remarked, 'We need to get those guys down to school to sort our pitch out.'

'I reckon,' Megs replied. 'They'd be there for a year doing it though!'

The banter (and hot dog eating) continued until the first sight of the returning players brought the crowd to its feet. Led out in two lines by the referees, they strode purposefully into the arena. Some players had faces like stone (you could see them on the big screen), and others smiled confidently as they waved to the crowd. One or two skipped every now and then as they walked. Each of them had a ball tucked under one arm.

The teams split up to go through their final preparation, and the Sydney players ran towards the stands with the balls and began booting them into the crowd.

The star of the Sydney team was a little Brazilian called Juninho, whom Megs had seen play for Middlesbrough when they played Liverpool a few years ago (Juninho had been good, but not good enough to stop the Reds winning). Today, his little legs ran to the sideline near the halfway before he stopped, looked around, then sent his ball high into the crowd... directly towards the Vootball Kids on the second tier. It spun through the air, closer and closer. And closer. It was coming straight to them.

Max was the first to react and shoved his way into position to catch it. Jed was beside him, and tried to lean across, but it made no difference. Max had been practising catching crosses ever since his mistake against the Sharks, and his training didn't fail him. He easily grabbed the ball above everyone else, then quickly tucked it under his arm, and pumped the air with his other fist. Down on the ground, Juninho gave a little wave, then sprinted off.

Jed and the other Kids around Max jostled and punched him good-naturedly. Even the parents joined in the fun. When they all calmed down, Max examined the ball, and was thrilled to discover that the *whole Sydney FC team had signed it!* For the remainder of the game, he didn't let the ball leave his grasp – even taking it with him to the toilet at half-time.

Melbourne Victory won the kick-off, and as they (and the packed stadium) awaited the referee's whistle to get the game underway, Mr Morrison leaned forward to get his son's attention. 'Too bad we have to go for a team in blue, but you've got to admit, this is the real thing, huh?'

Megs nodded in agreement, then heard the whistle blow to start the game. As he turned back towards the action, he caught a glimpse of Atti's face. The old man's eyes were fixed intently on the pitch, but were glistening with a hint of tears. Megs wondered how many long years had passed since he'd last seen live professional football.

Val didn't go to the game, which was a shame because her first live game would've been a ripper. Sydney had led 1–0 for most of the game, but, if they were honest, would have to admit they were lucky to be in that position. Melbourne had dominated throughout, and had drawn level near the end through some Archie Thompson magic (he then sprinted to the corner flag to do his boxing celebration). After that, Sydney had held on desperately, and with the help of the left goalpost had kept the score to 1–1.

Instead, Val had obviously spent some time on the internet, because Megs had received a group email from her when he arrived home after pizza and Coke with the gang. It was addressed to all the Vootball Kids.

GET THESE!!

Following up all those crazy-looking things you were doing the other day at training, Get THESE!

- In the 1994 World Cup, Nigerian Finidi George crawled to a corner flag, lifted his leg, and pretended to wee all over it like a dog! Most of his team-mates then followed along to join in the fun. Imagine if we all did that against the Sharks – led by Jed!

- In 1993, Celestine Babayaro of Chelsea injured himself twice by doing backflips. Club management threatened to whack him with some huge fines if he did it again.

- During the 90s, Lee Sharp of Man United used to pull out the corner flag and sing into it like a microphone while dancing like Elvis Presley.

- Fans in a village in Bolivia were so excited with a win over Uruguay, they didn't see one of their houses burning down nearby – set on fire by fireworks from the celebrations. By the time they noticed, most of the village had burned down!

- In 1998, the mascots of Wolverhampton Wanderers (another Wanderers… wonder how many there are??)

and Bristol City got into a big fight after a goal. Wolfie (Wolverhampton's mascot) was over-celebrating, so the Cat and three Pigs (the weird mascots of Bristol) beat him up! They all got sacked by their clubs.

- In 1994, the captain of Birmingham City was suspended for playing a trumpet while celebrating a goal. He was handed the instrument by a fan from the stands... and it wasn't even the captain that scored!

Here are the Wanderers I could find (pros only):
- Bolton Wanderers (England)
- Wycombe Wanderers (England)
- Wolverhampton Wanderers (England)
- Bray Wanderers (Ireland)

And how cool is THIS... A team just called 'Wanderers' won the first FA Cup in 1872 (no crossbars or nets). They were a bunch of players from private schools and universities. 2000 people watched the game that is now watched by millions and millions on TV and 100,000 at the ground. They won the comp 5 times! The ORIGINAL Wanderers!!!

There was also another email from Val, this time just to Megs and Paloma, entitled, 'What Do You Reckon?'

Hi guys,

I've been thinking and I reckon we need the Western Region Board to make a decision about the wording of the laws, otherwise we'll never know if Abda can play again. Or anyone else who wears a headscarf.

I know she doesn't want to make a fuss, but all this is killing her, I'm sure of it.

Val was right. Abda had loved watching the Sydney vs Melbourne game, and everyone could see how emotional she was when she said she wouldn't play the next match against Brenthill while the Western Region Board were making their decision on her headscarf. She was willing to sacrifice herself to make sure the team didn't lose another three points on her behalf.

Megs read on:

So I think we use the media. I think we need to go to the Board and tell them we'll use the media to make them all look bad. It's a bit mean to make a threat, but I can't see any other way, and something has to be done.

Paloma was obviously online as well.

G'day Val and Megs,

Ur right Val. It killed Abda to say she wouldn't play on Wednesday, but she still had so much fun at the game today. No way the Sharks would admit to setting the whole thing up against Trengal, even if they did. Getting the Board to change the rules – or at least make sure the refs don't interpret the rules like that loser against Trengal – is the only way.

But how do we do it?

Pal

Thirteen | Team-mates United

'*Could all the people involved in the soccer match against Brenthill Catholic this afternoon please now make their way to the front gate. Good luck, Wanderers!*'

As soon as the announcement started, Megs began packing up. By the time the announcement ended, he was already making his way out of the door. He was extra-excited this afternoon.

'Where are you going so fast, Edward?' asked Miss Sheather, her voice stopping Megs in his tracks. 'I know you've got a match, but you could at least show the class and me some courtesy and wait to be excused! You can't just go running in and out of the classroom when you feel like it!'

Megs liked Miss Sheather, but she did sometimes tend to exaggerate. And he also got the impression that she wasn't particularly happy about students in her class leaving to play sport once a week.

'Sorry, Miss Sheather. May I be excused?' he asked sheepishly. Miss Sheather gave a quick nod, and Megs scooted out the door, with Paloma not far behind. When they got outside, Paloma gave Megs a little punch on the arm, and zoomed off ahead to the waiting bus.

Megs called out as she ran, 'Make sure you, me and Val are sitting together on the bus. I've had an idea.'

'So, spill it.' Val and Paloma had squished in next to Megs, forcing him up against the window.

Megs answered Paloma's demand as directly as it was asked. 'Get a petition.'

Silence (except, of course, for the racket on the bus from the rest of the Vootball Kids).

So Megs continued, hardly stopping to breathe. 'If three Kids knock on the Board's door and say we aren't happy and that they need to change the rules, we aren't going to get far. But if we take a heap of signatures, it's different. And on top of that, we should fire up the newspapers and media to put even more pressure on the Board. Like you said, Val, the papers and telly keep wanting some stuff from us, so let's give it to 'em… just like when we asked Atti to coach us and he said no. We did something about it, and he ended up saying yes.' Megs was puffed.

'Yeah, you're probably right,' Paloma replied, slumping back into the seat with a thump as she thought about the task ahead. 'We'll get nowhere if we just talk about it. A petition will take some work though.'

'Look at the lovebirds,' joked Jed as he leaned into the conversation. 'Two girlfriends, Megs? Can't make up your mind?'

'Good one, Jed. Very clever,' Paloma replied sarcastically.

'Actually, we were trying to find a way for Abda to play again.' Val was looking Jed straight in the eyes, and obviously meant business.

Suddenly she stood up in the middle of the bus, yelling above the din: 'EVERYONE! CAN I HAVE A SEC PLEASE?'

Pretty quickly, everyone stopped what they were doing. Val continued, 'I know bringing this up now isn't going to help you prepare for the game, but this is more important.' Everyone was listening – including Atti (although he pretended to be asleep).

'In the last few days, Paloma, Megs and I have discovered some things about the Sharks and what happened to Abda, and reckon there's only one way to fix it. We've gotta go to the top.' Val spoke clearly and loudly as she explained what they had discovered. Not all the Kids understood straight away, but they were certainly interested.

Megs got onto his knees on his seat and faced his team-mates. Atti remained 'asleep', but was as interested as the rest of them, Megs felt sure. He took up the story, 'We reckon the only way to get anything changed is to make the Western Region Board change it. Let's make 'em change the rules so Abda can play.' He looked around the bus hopefully.

'But what are we supposed to do?' Jed asked, frowning. He was one of the angriest about what had been happening, but it was his nature to be sceptical.

Megs rolled on. 'Get a petition to take to them. You know –' he thought he'd better explain what a petition was, just in case '– get heaps of signatures.' Most of them were nodding. 'And get Val to write to the papers and email the radio, and all that.'

The bus bounced along the road to their match, but the match was the furthest thing from everyone's mind. Megs kept one eye on Atti, sitting very still at the front. He wondered if the old coach was secretly listening.

'How's that going to help, man? Why would they listen to us?' This time it was Max.

'They might not listen to one or two of us,' Val said, 'but they'll listen if we take heaps of signatures.'

'Why don't we organise a protest or something? The papers would LOVE that!' Angelique was obviously on board. 'You know, like when all those people protested about going to the Iraq war. Or when 100,000 people marched over the Harbour Bridge for the Aborigines.'

'Yeah. My dad went on strike a couple of months ago to protest because the workers didn't like some new regulations,' added Mitch. 'Maybe we could do something like that?'

'Who's gonna care if we strike, man? Striking from soccer will just lose us more points!' Jed pointed out.

'A strike from school would be cool!' chirped Max.

'I know!' It was Paloma's turn to get on her feet, swaying with the movement of the bus. 'Let's get as many people as possible to the next Board meeting. We can make signs and stuff, to let them know we're serious. We can take as many signatures as possible, and get TV cameras there as well! They'll HAVE to listen to us then!' Paloma's excitement was infectious. And it was a good idea.

'Cool!' exclaimed Adam. 'I'm in. Do we just get signatures on a piece of paper or something?'

'I'll print something up,' replied Val. 'We have to state our petition first, at the top of every page. Then if we all collect some signatures and get people to the next meeting, it might just work. Now we also need to find out when the next meeting is.'

Just then, Atti stood up at the front of the bus, removed his hat, rubbed the back of his neck, and said nothing for what seemed like minutes. The buzz in the bus didn't take long to die down.

His moustache danced a little, and his mouth creaked open. 'I've been sitting up there trying to sleep, but excited little voices keep me awake. But I know something to help. I know next meeting is next Monday in the State Football Federation offices. Under one week. Not long. But you kids remember... I not hear one word you lot say. Yes? Not one word. I not know anything about any of this, yes?'

He sat back down, and looked out the front window. From the back of the bus, an ovation erupted.

The sound of cheering from the Vootball Kids' bus arrived before the bus itself, so full of beans was the team. They spilled out carrying their bags, and milled around until they were shown their changing rooms. Once inside, Atti had his work cut out to focus his team back on the game at hand rather than on all the political scheming that had begun on the bus.

Once the balls were out and the warm-up drills were underway, however, the Wanderers began to switch on. Three points were vital to keep in touch with the Sharks, and with only three games to go in the season, any loss from here on would be extremely costly.

As the team re-entered the change rooms five minutes before the kick-off, a couple of vans with big satellite dishes on their roofs arrived. There were a number of people standing by themselves, speaking into small recording machines, and more people in suits than at other games they'd played. It was the first game after the 'Headscarf Incident' as some of the papers were calling it, and public interest was obviously still high.

Val was already in the rooms, notebook and pencil at the ready to hear Atti's speech. Megs sat next to her, and as he did, she leaned over and whispered, 'We'll have no problems getting the media interested – see the vans and reporters out there already, and Abda's not even playing! And there are some people here from the Board, too – I've seen them before.' Megs only nodded. It was all very interesting, but there was a game to be played.

'Miss Val. Please no reporting now. We have game to be ready for.' Atti had his game face on.

But before he could say any more, Abda's face poked around the changing-room doors. She hadn't come on the bus because she wasn't playing in the match, so she'd organised a lift to the ground straight after school.

'Abda! So cool that you made it in time!' Paloma was smiling from ear to ear.

'Can I come in, Atti?' Abda was nervous. 'There's a lot of people want to speak to me out there... maybe I should've stayed in the car with Dad.'

'Can you come in? 'COURSE you come in. You Vootball Kid, and you the one everyone been talking about all week.' Abda immediately looked a bit sheepish, despite Atti's good intentions in trying to make her feel welcome. She obviously hated to think of people speaking about her.

Atti continued, 'It's been big week, and everyone very proud of you all. At school, at training, in front of cameras. Everything. So good on Abda and good on all of you. Very brave, Abda. But for next minutes, you only think about the football.' He picked up a battered old ball to make his point. 'You not think about Abda. You not think about TV cameras. You not even think about the trip to England. Because if you thinking of the ball and thinking of your position, if you run and run, and if you light on your feet, three points will be yours. You not do that, and three points will not be yours. Easy, yes?' Atti smiled encouragingly.

The Vootball Kids all clapped and yelled, 'C'mon Wanderers!' as they stood up, ready to go. Atti limped around the room and shook everyone's hand to wish them luck. Abda was doing the same, patting her team-mates on the back and giving encouragement. She wished she was running out there with them, but at least she still felt like part of the gang.

It was Ivan's turn to be captain that day. 'Everyone ready?' he called out. 'Let's do it!' With that, he led the team out of the rooms, jogging past three or four cameramen and journalists and onto the field. He looked even taller than usual.

As they made it to the pitch, Megs heard familiar voices. 'C'mon, Megs! C'mon, son!' and 'Good luck, Megsy!' His parents were there to surprise him.

Looking over his shoulder, Megs could see a couple of the journalists going straight for Abda. Her dad was there to escort her away – probably back to their car to watch the game in peace.

Despite Atti's instructions before the game, Megs couldn't help but think of their plans to have Abda play again. It wasn't right that she should have so many hassles to even watch them play. They had to make things right.

But the thought was fleeting, quickly interrupted by the referee's whistle. As soon as the ball was kicked off by the Brenthill strikers, Megs thought of nothing else.

The ball was like water for a fish, sky for an aeroplane, or gold for an old miner. He just needed to get it! He wanted to touch it, and in the words of Atti, make it dance. And that meant that anyone else who had it had better look out!

Pennendale were in good form from start to finish, and easily accounted for Brenthill 4–0. Megs led the way, scoring two goals (aeroplane celebration for both) and setting up another. But it was his general play that made him stand out. No-one could get near him as he ducked, wove and darted about every centimetre of the ground. He may have been one of the smallest players out there, but he knew he was head and shoulders above the rest. The other goal-scorers were Paloma (who ran full pelt towards Abda's car after scoring, pointing and waving to her as she went, while inside the car, Abda screamed her head off) and Ivan (who went for the shirt-over-the-head and run-around-like-a-madman celebration. None of the Wanderers had ever seen him move so fast!)

After the match, news filtered through that the Sharks had also won, though the result was a much closer 1–0. And they had squeezed home with only minutes to spare. Still, the Sharks topped the table with only two games to go. If both teams won their next game, it would come down to the last game of the season between the two rivals, and Pennendale would have to win it. A draw wouldn't be enough.

Megs's whole body was tingling after the match. He knew he'd played well. He told himself: We can still do it. We just have to win two more games!

ROUND 16				
CLUB	W	L	D	Pts
Southside Sharks	12	2	2	38
Pennendale Wanderers	11	2	3	36
Hills Rockets	8	3	5	29

Fourteen | People Power

'Come on, Megs, we're going out!' Mr Morrison was in another one of his 'glass half full' moods, and Mrs Morrison was also pretty pumped. Megs, on the other hand, wanted to stay right where he was. There was scheming to do.

'Oh ma-an… I'm busy!' he replied.

'Busy? It's the weekend and you're eleven years old – how busy can you be?' his mum asked.

'Busy enough. Why can't I just stay home?'

'You're not staying home,' Mr Morrison replied quickly. 'And what are you doing there? Doesn't look like homework. Come on, you'll want to come…'

Megs didn't look convinced, so his mum continued. 'True, you'll REALLY want to be in on this, I promise.'

'I'm happy you two want to make the most of the sun and blah, blah, blah, but I'm happy staying here doing this.' Megs was sticking to his guns.

'Anfield…' Mrs Morrison blurted out.

Megs screwed up his face, confused.

'Anfield…' she repeated, smiling.

Megs looked to his dad for help, but Mr Morrison just smiled mysteriously and raised his eybrows.

'What are you talking abou–? ARE WE GETTING A DOG?' It hit Megs like a long ball to the forehead.

All his parents could do was laugh.

'Are we?' Megs was on his feet now, his previous efforts at the computer forgotten. 'Are we getting the dog?'

'Well, we thought we'd have a look...' said Mr Morrison.

'We ARE getting the dog!! We ARE! Does that mean we're definitely staying as well?' It was Megs's turn to be pumped.

'It doesn't mean we're *definitely* staying, but it means we're going to give it a serious go. *Now* do you want to come with us?' Mrs Morrison grinned widely.

Megs was already shutting the computer down. Scheming and politicking with the Vootball Kids could wait.

The three of them piled into the car, all speaking at least 20 per cent louder than usual. The earlier arguments about small dog versus big dog had never been resolved, so Mr and Mrs Morrison thought it would be better to go to the Lost Dogs Home and see what happened when they got there.

And when they did get there, it was tough. So many dogs that needed a home! So much cuteness, so many wagging tails. But only one home on offer.

The Morrisons were shown around, then the owners of the home let out a few of the pups to yap around the

Morrisons' heels, run around, wrestle with each other, and generally show off.

But one little ball of puppy muscle waggled straight in between Megs's legs and stayed there. His dark brown tail shook like crazy, and his deep brown eyes stared straight into Megs's. He twisted and turned through Megs's feet, and the white patch over his left eye made him look like he was constantly trying to wink.

Mr and Mrs Morrison were playing with a range of puppies, patting them all and trying to gauge their personalities. Finding Anfield was tough!

Megs had the little brown puppy in his arms and was rubbing under its ears. The dog's long tongue was not in proportion to its small body, but it was just as active, licking Megs all over the face.

'This isn't easy, is it?' asked Mrs Morrison as she turned in the direction of her son. 'Or maybe it is...' She laughed at Megs, who was now basically wearing the little dog as a hat. Even the puppy seemed to be grinning from ear to ear.

'This is him! Or her... Whatever, this is Anfield!' Megs was ecstatic.

'I'm starting to see that!' Mrs Morrison smiled.

The owner of the home confirmed that little Anfield was actually a Staffordshire bull terrier, and was certainly not a boy dog. She was just three months old, and had been found wandering some lanes behind the Pennendale Shops, eating what she could from rubbish bins. She was very sick when they'd found her, but in the two weeks she'd been at the home, she'd recovered quickly, and become one of the staff's favourites. But more importantly, she now seemed to have chosen Megs as *her* favourite!

When they got little Anfield back to 20 Valetta Avenue, Megs realised how different the 'vibe' of their house would be from now on. In fact, it already was. Anfield was the centre of attention, and Mrs Morrison was entirely smitten. Megs hadn't seen his mother so happy in ages.

Not until Anfield finally went to sleep in the afternoon (with the help of a hot water bottle and a ticking clock to recreate the comfort of her mother's warmth and heartbeat), did Megs remember the Vootball Kids' plan. Quickly, he went back online to see how things were progressing.

The forum threads were getting bigger and bigger, and everyone he knew seemed to be online, chatting, messaging and Skyping. Their plan was taking shape.

The plan they'd decided on was so simple that it seemed almost too easy. But Val and Paloma were convinced it would work, and Megs was smart enough to agree with them.

After the last game against Brenthill, Val wrote her match report as usual, but also spent time on another article entitled 'The Real Story'. It was emotional and direct, outlining everything they had discovered about the situation with Abda. She raised everything she knew the media wanted to hear, and didn't hold back. This was no time for taking the middle road. The article finished with a demand that as many people as possible turned up at the next Western Region Board meeting to protest. Only the weight of numbers would change anything. Only people power would get Abda playing again.

While waiting for the newspapers to pick up Val's article, Megs, Paloma, Val and all the Vootball Kids emailed and SMSed everyone they knew, sending them a link to the online version.

It worked. The chat rooms and forums Megs was looking at were chock-full, so he began to feel pretty happy with himself. At the rate they were going, the Board meeting in a couple of days would be overrun by protesters. The Trengal Tigers were being especially supportive, and seemed to be as fired up as the Wanderers. Even parents and non-football people were joining in. And increasingly, people from overseas were sending through their support. *I wonder if I should get Woody and the boys involved?* Megs thought.

There was a knock at the door; Mrs Morrison went to answer it with Anfield skipping along at her heels. 'Oh, hi girls! Everything OK?'

Megs could hear the surprise in his mum's voice, so got up from the computer to go to the door.

Val and Paloma were there, along with Abda. All three of them went nuts at the sight of the newest member of the Morrison clan, who bounded out to say hello. They stooped to play with the furry brown ball while she nibbled at their hands and pawed at Abda's gown.

'She's so cute!' Paloma spoke for all of them as she hugged Anfield close to her neck.

'I'll leave you to it, then,' said Mrs Morrison as Megs

approached. He immediately wished he had his ball with him – it was weird having the three girls at his front door, with or without a cute puppy to deflect attention. Val and Abda had never even been to his house before, so something was up.

The four of them went outside, and sat on the front lawn to talk.

'Cool puppy!' Abda said. 'What's its name?'

'Anfield,' Megs replied.

'You're kidding!' Paloma laughed, before explaining to Val and Abda, 'Anfield is where Liverpool play. It's the name of their stadium.'

'And you called your dog after a stadium?' Val was constantly amazed by how much some people loved football. It was just a game after all! But then, as she started to speak, she understood that wasn't actually true.

'We came to talk about the protest,' she said. Abda started fiddling with her watch, not meeting anyone's eyes.

Megs stabbed a stick into the dirt enthusiastically. 'Isn't it great! All those people getting behind us. Just wait until it's in the papers tomorrow. We'll then have the TV cameras back, and they won't be able to back down. Everyone'll be talking about it!'

'Actually, that's a bit of a problem…' Val said a bit sheepishly. Abda started biting her top lip.

Val continued, 'Yeah, the plan's working, and it's taking on a life of its own.' *Then why isn't she looking happy?* Megs wondered. 'Thing is, we didn't think it

ALL through.'

Abda scratched her elbow and stared at the ground, scuffing her shoes in the grass.

Paloma took up the story. 'Thing is, we didn't really ask Abda about any of this. We got all excited and thought we were doing the right thing, and now it's rolling on out of our control. Abda wasn't on the bus to the game that day, and we didn't ask her about it.'

Abda then spoke, quietly at first, then with increasing confidence. 'It's great how you want to do all this, and how you all didn't play against Trengal, but it's too much. I don't want to draw attention to myself or my family, and we just want it to go away – not get worse.'

'But don't you want to play again?' Megs asked.

'Yeah, but all this is crazy! I don't want to explain myself to the TV and all that. And I don't want to be the main target at a protest, like some sort of freak show.'

Megs hadn't thought of it like that.

'When Abda told us all this, we felt horrible,' said Val. 'So we thought you should know, too.'

Megs was quiet for a moment, so Val continued. 'The last thing we wanted was to hurt you, Abda.'

'I know,' Abda replied. 'And that's what makes all this so hard. I want to play, and I'm happy you've done all this, but I also want it all to go away.'

Megs spoke up. 'Life doesn't always fit inside a picture frame,' he remarked. 'That's one of Dad's sayings, and I only just get it now. You know, it's not always pretty like a picture on a wall. Like – you can't always play great football, but as long as you get the three points, who cares, right?'

'And...?' Paloma didn't quite get it, so asked the question for all the girls.

'Well, if Abda wants to play, then this is the only way.' He turned to Abda. 'True, we should've talked with you first, and we're sorry, but it'll be worth it. If we win the next two games, then we take the League title away from those Sharks, and get the trip to England. Surely that's worth a bit of inconvenience!'

'What do you think?' Paloma asked Abda.

'It's all too full-on, that's what I think!' Abda wailed.

'Well, how about you don't have to say or do anything?' Val didn't want to give up just yet either. 'You don't have to come to the protest or do anything in front of the cameras and all that. You just lie low for a week or so, and let us cause the fuss. We can say it's all our fault.'

'Which it is...' added Megs with a smile.

'And if it doesn't work?' Abda wondered aloud.

'If it doesn't work, then we'll regroup!' Val replied.

'It'll work,' said Megs. 'It'll work, and we'll win. We'll stick it to those Sharks, and we'll go to England. And you'll be a part of it.'

'And anyway,' said Val thoughtfully, 'The media is probably right you know... it's a bigger issue than just winning football. Now we're also fighting for people's rights to their own customs and beliefs.' There was silence for a minute.

'OK,' Abda sighed reluctantly, 'but keep me out of it. And if nothing changes before the next game, you're not allowed to forfeit. And I'll stay home this time to keep out of the way. And… thank you.' She was close to tears. The three girls stood and hugged, but Megs stayed sitting on the grass. It was weird how girls hugged each other all the time.

By the time the Western Region Board meeting came around, the petition had over 2 300 names on it. Each had been collected by the Vootball Kids and added to one big list. There were seventeen forum threads, and twelve newspaper articles from around the world. Talk-back radio in Sydney had discussed it for over twenty minutes, and even interviewed Val about it during recess. Abda had been kept out of the limelight, but it was turning into a bigger deal than any of them had imagined.

Mr Simon Prior from the Western Region Board (and organiser of the trip) had been interviewed a few times. And even though he had said he wished there wasn't so much fuss, he had also said how impressed he was with the spirit of the Pennendale team.

There was one quote in particular that gave Megs hope: *'I don't know if it'll get them anywhere with the rules the way they are, but they've certainly made the Board take notice. After all, we're all about encouraging kids to play, and we need to do what we can to make sure that happens.'*

The meeting was set to start at 8pm, and by 7pm no-one was there except Paloma, Mr Mendez, Val and her elder brother, Mr and Mrs Morrison, Megs and Anfield.

The protest signs they'd all made looked very lonely out in front of the big office building.

By 7.30pm, some more of the Vootball Kids had arrived, and the atmosphere began to get more jovial.

By 7.40pm, the place was alive. People had seemingly come out of the woodwork, TV cameras were being set up, and photographers were looking for the best angles.

The first Board member arrived at 7.45pm. She managed to get past the crowd with a number of 'no comments', walking as quickly as possible.

When the rest of the Board arrived between 7.50pm and 8pm, they didn't find it so easy. The crowd in front of the building was so big it had spilt into the street, blocking traffic. Protest chants were following traditional football tunes, and were getting louder.

'We're all here to have our say
You should all let Abda play!'

And: '*Everywhere we go-o, people want to kno-ow, whoo-oo-oo we a-a-are! So we tell them, we're the Wanderers – the mighty, mighty Wanderers! And we a-a-are, the best by f-a-ar. THAT'S who we are!'* Even the Trengal Tigers joined in that one.

Of course, the TV cameras loved every minute, and each Board member that was forced to push through the crowd to enter the building was left with no doubt that the protesters were serious.

Megs, Paloma and Val wondered what would happen next. All their attention had been focused on the protest, which had so far worked brilliantly. It was almost like a runaway train, in fact. But what would come of it?

At 8.15pm, their wondering came to an end. The door opened and Simon Prior stepped out. Immediately the crowd quietened, although a few of the protesters towards the back continued their chants, not realising that something might be about to happen. 'Could the organisers of tonight's event, please come forward?' he called. Cameras clicked and flashes flashed. Megs, Paloma and Val looked at each other, and shrugged.

Mr Mendez broke the spell. 'Well, this is it – off you go!' he gave Paloma a little shove. 'See what you can do!' he smiled proudly.

Mr and Mrs Morrison looked at Megs and nodded. Val's elder brother pointed towards the door, stepping aside to gesture Val forward.

All three Vootball Kids edged nervously towards Mr Prior and the open door. The raucous cheering in the background hit new levels – if that was possible!

But Mr Prior was a friendly sort of man, with a round face beneath thinning hair. In his polo shirt and jeans he seemed very relaxed, considering the situation. 'Ahhh, so you're the Three Musketeers creating all the fuss, huh! Well done! It's about time you came on upstairs, I think. Let's talk.' He looked over to the adults to see if they were going to accompany the three of them, but each of them waved their hands in front of them to indicate, 'Go ahead. They're on their own.'

The Kids would have to do the next bit by themselves.

'Everyone, let me introduce Paloma, Val and Edward
– but everyone calls him Megs.' Megs was impressed.
Val had introduced Megs to Mr Prior as 'Edward', but
he already knew his nickname. 'They're the Pennendale
Wanderers kids.'

The room was bright and reminded Megs of a hotel
foyer or even a hospital waiting room. The difference was
that there were pennants and trophies lining the walls,
and there was a big, shiny table right in the middle of
the room. At the table were five people (apart from Mr
Prior), all of whom were wearing suits. In his tracksuit
pants and Liverpool shirt, Megs felt like he was wearing
normal clothes at a fancy dress party.

Mr Prior saw him scanning the walls. 'Impressive stuff,
isn't it? Not quite like the Anfield boardroom and trophy
cabinet back in Liverpool, though.' Megs was starting to
like this man – he knew his stuff. 'And this is the one that
you might have your hands on soon.' Mr Prior walked
towards a long, skinny cup that had two little handles
and a thick, black base. In truth, it looked as though a
stiff breeze might blow it over, but it gave Megs a flutter
to see it, just steps away, shining and so very real. He
glanced at Paloma, and they both smiled.

Bang, bang, bang!

An old man with glasses resting on top of his balding
head, had hit a little hammer on the table. 'Right, then,
that's all very nice, but let's keep things moving along,
shall we?' He rubbed his red bow tie between forefinger
and thumb, and looked around the room with an air of
authority.

'We all know why we're here,' Mr Bow Tie continued. 'These three kids have created all manner of fuss –' his arm swept towards the window and the people in the street '– and now we have to do something about it.'

'One Atti Czibar, there's only one Atti Czibar. One Atti Cziibaaarrr, there's only one Atti Czibar!'

Megs smiled as he heard the song from below, but Val looked sternly forward. Mr Prior remained standing next to the three Vootball Kids, as Mr Bow Tie pushed on.

'We've had hassles from the media, people sending us letters, and even calling me at home! *At home!* It is not something any of us are happy about, and it's something that has to stop. You three kids started it, so we'd like to know how you are going to stop it.'

Was this guy serious? Megs frowned as his brain ticked over.

Val, on the other hand, leapt into action. 'How *we* are going to stop it!' There was an edge to her voice. 'These people aren't here because of us, they're here because of the rules, because of fairness! They're here because we all think Abda should be allowed to play. In fact, anyone wearing a headscarf should be able to play.' Val finished off much calmer than she had started off, and her words seemed to have some impact.

'Well, you shouldn't have gone to the media and stirred up all this fuss. It doesn't look good. You should've just come to us,' Mr Bow Tie was sticking to his guns. The other four Board members shuffled in their seats.

'The media came to us. There were already online forums before we had even discussed any of this. We just made the most of it. And do you really think you'd be listening to us right now if we didn't have all these people behind us?' Val really was SO GOOD at this stuff!

'Bravo, Val. Bravo.' Mr Prior was as impressed as Paloma and Megs. He was still standing next to them – none of them had been invited to sit.

It was the turn of a lady with big hair and tan make-up to say her piece. 'Your passion for fairness must be commended, and we are certainly not here to stop people playing. The more kids that play the better. But we have to follow the FIFA rules; if you'd read them you'd know that –'

Paloma jumped in. 'Well, we have read them, and they don't say anything about headscarves. They mention jewellery, colours and safety, but they don't mention headscarves!'

Ms Big Hair continued, 'No not specifically, they don't, you're right. But if a referee thinks something is dangerous, then it's his call.'

'Don't you think it's strange that this incident happened in that game and at that time?' Paloma was taking a leaf out of Val's book and Megs was amazed by her courage. 'The Sharks knew all about it. They were onto the ref about it before the game. One of their dads used to be on this Board, and that ref works with him!'

'I don't know what you're trying to accuse us of, young lady!' Mr Bow Tie was going red in the face.

'OK, OK, let's calm down, everyone.' Mr Prior extended his arms to include the whole room.

'Gimme a P – P! Gimme an E – E!. Gimme an N – N!

and once again! – N!...' rang out from downstairs.

Mr Prior continued quietly, 'Whether or not the Sharks and their parents had something to do with it is not really the issue. We'll never know if that's true or not, so let's deal with what we can.' He turned to the Board members. 'The headscarf issue is what we have to deal with. When it's all broken down, we need to decide whether we make a ruling that people in headscarves can play. Can we take a stand like all those people out there?' He gestured towards the chanting crowd down in the street.

Yep, Mr Prior WAS a good bloke, Megs thought.

'Is there anything else you children would like to add before we ask you to leave so we can make a decision?' Ms Big Hair seemed to have calmed down quite a lot.

'Well, we figure it shouldn't be this hard. You don't have to change the rules – you just have to tell the refs that headscarves aren't dangerous. Maybe recommend that they be firmly tied, and not using pins. It's never been a problem before now, so if the refs don't get pressure from other teams, they can let Abda play.' Megs and Paloma nodded as Val spoke clearly and strongly.

'And what about you, Edward Megs?' Mr Bow Tie was still holding his little hammer.

Edward Megs indeed. Megs couldn't think of anything new to say, but seeing he'd been asked, he added a few words. 'Abda is a good player and she's a part of our team. It's not fair that she can't play, and it's not fair she has to go through all this.' It wasn't the greatest of speeches, but Megs felt better from having said it anyway.

'OK, thank you. We know your thoughts and thank you for the effort. We'll let you know soon.' It was Ms Big Hair again. Mr Bow Tie seemed to be lost in his own thoughts. Mr Prior ushered Megs, Paloma and Val out of the room, and once they were outside, he gave them a wink. 'Well done, kids, well done,' he said. 'You're doing great stuff on the pitch, and you're doing great stuff off it as well. Hopefully the Board will make the right decision…'

By the time Mr Prior came back down into the street, there were only about forty protesters left – as well as a few of the hardier reporters and camera operators. It had been one-and-a-half hours since Megs, Paloma and Val had left the boardroom, and everyone was starting to feel tired and flat.

Throughout the evening, Val had taken about seven calls from Abda. One time, she held the phone up towards the crowd as they chanted, *'There's no way, there's no way, there's no way she shouldn't play!'*

The Vootball Kids heard Val say, 'Don't cry, Abda. All these people wanted to fight for you – and for fairness. It will all work out, you'll see.'

Finally Mr Prior came down to see the remaining protesters in the street. A hush fell over the crowd.

'Well,' he smiled, 'you should be congratulated. It's

the first time I can ever remember something getting decided on one night and in one meeting.'

Camera flashes were lighting up his face as he spoke.

'First, you should know that we can't change FIFA's rules. But what we can do is to write a letter to the refs to let them know our stance. We've decided that headscarves are not dangerous, so long as they are firmly and safely tied, and in our opinion wearing one shouldn't hinder anyone from playing this great game.'

Raucous cheers erupted. Val was already calling Abda on her mobile.

'But hang on, hang on,' Mr Prior continued, his arms outstretched, trying to quieten everyone down. 'Your next game is in four days. We'll get the letter written and sent, but after that it's still up to the referees. That's all we can do. So don't get too excited just yet.'

He was right. This decision wasn't a guarantee of anything.

But Mr Prior had more to say. 'And I would also ask you journos to respect what is happening here, and especially to respect what Abda is going through.'

Megs could see the other Board members looking down from the window above. Mr Bow Tie's podgy cheeks were red, but on the whole they looked pleased.

Down below, 'pleased' was an understatement. Mr Morrison put an arm around his son's shoulder as Mr Prior continued, 'And finally, I'd like to congratulate you all for taking a stand. Atti, no wonder you're so proud of your team. What is that you call them... the Vootball Kids?'

Atti smiled and nodded as the Vootball Kids erupted into cheers around him. No words were needed when everyone saw the pride and joy on his face.

The crowd began to clear, and as Megs, Paloma and Val left with their families, Paloma turned to the others and quietly said what they'd all been thinking: 'Now, let's stick it up those Sharks for real.'

Fifteen | Newfound Fame from Playing the Game

Match day against Fairfield arrived. It was the second-last game of the season, and four days after the protest at the Board meeting. And in those four days, the Vootball Kids' stand had dominated the sports reports in the newspapers, websites and radio stations. Virtually all comments were congratulatory, but if the Vootball Kids thought the fuss would die down now that the protest was over, they were wrong. They'd done too good a job in whipping up the frenzy.

Abda had been persuaded to come ready to play. She'd been in hiding for the last few days as she waited for the excitement to die down, and hadn't even been to school. And despite the fuss, still no-one knew whether she would be allowed to play. No-one knew who the ref would be, and what stance he would take. Val and Paloma had helped Abda to arrive at a positive attitude, but secretly she confessed she was terrified that today's match would be an embarrassing repeat of the showdown they'd had when they'd played Trengal a few weeks ago.

To add to the tension, the Sharks had won their game

3–0 the day before, and had done it in fine style. That result meant that if the Wanderers lost or even drew in this match, the title would be out of reach. The Sharks would be champions even if Pennendale beat them on the last day of the season.

Fairfield were at the low end of the table but the history of football is filled with surprise results and heartbroken favourites. The Wanderers were determined that they wouldn't be a part of that kind of history. They were determined to make their own history.

It was Pennendale's home game, but big Mr Jackson, the school Principal, had pulled a few strings and managed to get the use of a local State League team's ground instead of using their normal pitch in the park. Initially, Megs wasn't thrilled about the switch because they'd been so successful on their usual ground, and he didn't want to jinx it. But by the time their bus had reached the other ground, he'd changed his mind.

There was a small stadium down one side of the ground, and a covered standing area down the other. Fencing and advertising boards framed the pitch, and the lines were already marked - thick, white and classy. The nets were already up (a perfect box-shape to both of them) and the corner flags were brightly coloured and new, hanging limp in the warm, still air.

The bus drove through the gates, then pulled up behind the small stand. The Vootball Kids were strangely quiet as they surveyed the surroundings. The 'proper' ground seemed to emphasise the seriousness of the upcoming game, and the tension grew.

When the bus came to a standstill, Atti stood and faced his team. He looked stressed. Outside, Megs saw a couple of people with cameras slung around their necks, and notepads in their hands. Val was travelling with the team, and had seen them too. Quickly, she pulled out her own notepad, too.

Atti began to speak, and nerves made his words even more difficult to understand than usual. His habitual smile was non-existent. 'OK, Vootball Kids. You know what has to do today. I proud of you, very, no matter what happen, always.' His voice began to waver, 'The way you all…' The Vootball Kids shuffled uncomfortably in their seats, not knowing how to react to the emotions of their coach. The tension in the bus grew.

But then, Atti seemed to snap out of it. He stood taller, and gave a big smile. He had realised the emotional path he was on was only making things worse. It was coaching genius.

'Ahh, no matter, no matter.' His voice became strong. 'You already know all that emotion stuff. So, here is my NEW big speech before game. Ready?'

The Kids didn't know if they were ready or not. Atti was freaking them out a bit. He smiled broadly, then pushed on.

'A zoo-keeper approaches three boys standing near lions' cage in zoo, asks their names and what they are doing.

'The first boy say, "My name Tommy and I was trying to feed peanuts to the lions."

'Second boy say, "My name Billy and I was trying to

feed peanuts to lions, too."

'The third boy say, "My name is Peanuts."'

There was a confused pause, then all of a sudden, Jed snorted with laughter. Val couldn't help but giggle. From somewhere at the back of the bus, someone else joined in, and pretty soon the giggles turned into chuckles. And, like dominoes, the tension broke. A week of tension burst its banks and overflowed. Even Abda's stress-filled face loosened, and as soon as Paloma gave her a little nudge on the shoulder, she lost it too. She hadn't felt that good in weeks.

'Don't give up your day job, super-coach!' called out Max cheekily.

'OK, let's go get ready!' Atti led his troops out of the bus and straight into the change-rooms. It was just like on telly – the reporters wanted stories and the cameramen wanted photos. But the Vootball Kids clattered down the bus stairs and waved them away. They had a game to play.

And besides, everyone was laughing too much to give a half-decent interview.

The warm-up was lively and the team was feeling full of beans. No-one (not even Abda) gave the last week another thought once the warm-up began. Their collective mind was thinking only about the game.

But when the referee signalled for the team to return

to the change-rooms so he could check their equipment, the old tensions began to surface once more. Abda's father was standing near the entrance alongside a number of other parents, as the players walked past. *He looks tired,* Megs thought.

The team entered the dim, quiet change-rooms and sat expectantly. The earlier noise and banter had been replaced by a big silence. Would Abda be allowed to play?

The ref bustled into the room with a spring in his step, seemed to assess the situation, and commented cheerfully, 'Well, aren't you guys popular! There's more media out there than when David Beckham turned up to play in America!' The Vootball Kids smiled. The ref continued, 'I bet you're all nervous, but play the whistle and have a good game and everything will be fine.'

Then, he looked over to Abda, whose eyes were boring a hole into the floor. 'To me, you playing as part of this team is more important than all these debates going on. So good luck to you all, and well done for sticking together!'

A cheer erupted as if the game were already won. Paloma and Val jumped to hug Abda, who was smiling although her eyes were suspiciously bright.

Outside, murmurs turned to cheers (and some jeers from Sharks players watching from the stands) when the team ran out of the change-rooms and onto the pitch – with Abda, captain for the day, leading the way.

There was just no way they were going to lose that match. The Wanderers had been through too much and had too much energy to be contained by any opposition. They were playing with so much confidence and zest that even if Liverpool had been their opponents instead of the unfortunate Fairfield, the Vootball Kids would probably have given them a run for their money.

In the end, they won 4–0, but in truth it could've been seven. Fairfield didn't even have a chance, and Max was practically just a spectator in goals. In fact, he spent most of the second half chatting to some other Pennendale Primary kids who'd come to watch and were standing behind his goal.

Atti found it difficult to select the most valuable player in the match because everyone had been excellent. Paloma scored two of the four goals, with the Simpfenator and Ivie scoring one each. Megs had hit the post twice, and belted a free kick from outside the box right onto the crossbar. It had hit so hard that it rebounded back out to the edge of the penalty box!

Of course, most of the crowd's attention was on Abda throughout the match, and after a nervous start, she got better and better. It didn't take long before she was again moving around the pitch with her trademark grace and fancy footwork. She played the full match, and came off at the end red-faced and puffed, but very happy.

After the game, reporters made a beeline to her. All she said was, 'I'm really happy to be playing again and I'm glad that we won the game' – although her massive smile gave that away easily enough. Val put her notebook away and ran through the reporters to Abda to give her friend a mighty hug. They walked to the change-rooms together arm-in-arm, chattering at a million miles an hour as they relived the match.

Megs could've played another match right there and then, but they'd all have to wait until the big one now. Only one more match to win and they'd be off to England as champions. All they had to do was beat those Sharks. *We won't just beat them – we'll teach them a lesson!* Megs already had his game face on, and there was still a week to go.

Megs and Paloma hardly paused for breath on their way to school as they recounted the last match. They were getting very excited about how close they now were to winning the trip.

But when they turned the last corner and saw the school gates, both of them stopped, silent, in their tracks.

Across the top of the gate were blue streamers. On the noticeboard out the front, in big black letters, was written: 'Carn Our Wanderers, Atti's Vootball Kids!' – 'football' was even spelt with a 'v'!

When they walked in, Mr Jackson was there. His big Aussie voice boomed 'Well done!' as he gave Megs a hefty slap on the back. From somewhere, he'd got his hands on a Pennendale Wanderers tracksuit, and even though he was too big to zip it up, he was wearing it with obvious pride. 'Here's two of the heroes. Our little Englishman and our goal-scoring sensation. Well done! Great game, great game.'

There was no time to respond, however, because Max and Jed had just entered the school behind Megs and Paloma, and Mr Jackson had already moved on to welcome and congratulate them. Megs and Paloma stared at each other in surprise. A few months ago Mr Jackson hadn't even wanted a team, and now look at him!

It was pretty much the same story throughout the day. Students and teachers alike all wanted to talk about the latest win and about the upcoming game against the Sharks. Megs might not have got the hero's welcome he expected after their first game of the season against the Baystone Blues (even though he'd scored that hat-trick), but the school was making up for it now. The Vootball Kids were the new stars of Pennendale Primary – no longer a bunch of sporting outcasts kicking a ball around on a dusty patch of the schoolground.

The *Pennendale Press* was filled with stories about the team, about Atti, and about what was in store after victory in their next game. The main Sydney paper even had a story. It mostly focused on Abda being able to play again, but there was also a great group photo of the team after the match as they celebrated.

It seemed like half the world had gone online to congratulate the team (and Abda) in the forums. Megs had an inbox full of emails – including a couple from Woody and Stevie R back in England. 'Only one game to go' was the essence of both messages, but it gave Megs a real buzz to hear from his old friends.

For Megs, the attention was extra sweet. After all, not long ago he had been sitting by himself in the corner of the playground, lonely and missing his 'home'. Now, he was the talk of the school, and even the Principal wanted to say well done.

But he also knew that the job wasn't finished yet. And no matter how nice it was to be the centre of attention now, the glory would fast disappear if the Wanderers didn't win against the Sharks.

They just *had* to beat those Sharks.

ROUND 17				
CLUB	W	L	D	Pts
Southside Sharks	**13**	**2**	**2**	**41**
Pennendale Wanderers	12	2	3	39
Hills Rockets	9	3	5	32

Sixteen | The Big One

On the morning of the big match, Megs woke to snuffles and slobbers. It was the Morrisons' little dog Anfield with a thick blue ribbon around her collar, marked with a white number seven. Megs probably could've slept a bit longer, but he was happy to give Anfield a wrestle and a pat, and get the day underway.

'All ready to go, Anfield? You gonna bring us some more luck today?' Anfield gave a little yap, and Megs ruffled her ears once more. It was a crisp, clear Saturday morning, and he was buoyant.

Megs bounced out of his bedroom, dribbling his now well-worn Champions League football as he made his way along the passage. Anfield was snapping at his heels and ferreting for the ball as he went. The little puppy was certainly a determined defender.

Mr and Mrs Morrison were already up, and sitting at the kitchen table doing a quiz from the newspaper. Both of them were wearing blue shirts, with Megs's mum looking ridiculous in a blue-and-white striped beanie, complete with white pom-pom on the top. It had

"Bulldogs" written on it in large letters.

'Look what you've brought us to, Megs!' Mr Morrison looked up from the paper to greet his son. 'We're wearing blue! The proud Morrison family wears blue!' He laughed. 'But I just want you to know that our blood still runs red, OK? Don't you go getting any ideas…'

Mrs Morrison saw her son glance at her headwear, and explained, 'There aren't any Pennendale beanies, and I saw this in an op shop. I think it's actually for the Bulldogs rugby league team, but it should do the trick.'

By now, Mr Morrison had scraped his chair back and was on his feet. 'Right then, Megs, come and have a seat for breakfast.' But he was directing his son towards the couch in front of the TV – a definite no-no at breakfast time in the Morrison household.

Megs stood on the spot, not wanting to get sucked in to a trick. His dad could see his hesitation. 'Come on, it's a special treat for a special day,' he said, pointing to the best spot on the couch, and picking up the remote control. He clicked the button and the DVD player sprang into life. The music was instantly recognisable, as were the images. Megs didn't waste any time, and jumped onto the couch with a thud. His dad threw him the remote and said, 'Enjoy!'

The DVD was called 'Liverpool, Team of the Century' and focused on the eighties when Liverpool had won everything there was to win – and usually more than once. Megs wasn't even born during this time, but he loved this DVD. It was all about winning, and the Reds had done it in style back then. European Cups, FA Cups,

League titles – there was nothing they hadn't won. Terry McDermott was Megs's favourite player from the early eighties (though he still wasn't better than Gerrard), but the likes of Dalglish, Rush, Whelan, Grobbelar, Souness, Barnes and even an Aussie called Craig Johnston were also brilliant to watch. It was his favourite viewing before a big game.

Soon his mum brought over a bowl with five Weet-bix drowning in milk and sugar, along with a freshly squeezed orange juice. This was the life.

Half an hour later, Mrs Morrison took Megs's empty bowl and told him they had to leave in fifteen minutes. His bag had been packed the night before (you don't want to rush these things on match day), and before long he was ready to roll. He'd even brushed his teeth.

The last few days had passed as if Megs was walking through mud. Slow, hard work. A bit like the waiting before Christmas Day or his birthday, time seemed to tick more and more slowly. He had been trying to keep a lid on the emotion and excitement, but now that the match was so close, he felt ready to explode.

There was a fair chance that Mr and Mrs Morrison had spoken about other things in the last few days, but Megs couldn't be exactly sure. He couldn't recall them arguing lately, and his dad seemed to have been around a bit more. But there had really been only one topic spinning around in Megs's brain… beating the Sharks and winning the Championship.

The game had been moved to a Saturday to allow as many family and friends as possible to come along and watch. If it hadn't been the League decider, it would've been played after school on Friday, but there was so much interest in the match that the Western Region Board made the decision early in the week to change the day, and had been busy ever since notifying supporters by every possible means, from websites and phone calls to posters in shop windows. Everyone knew about this game.

In the lead-up, most of the attention was on Pennendale. They were the sentimental favourites to win, but even with the weight of public support behind them, most people agreed that the Sharks were probably the better team. But either way, it was going to be a close-run thing, and a large crowd was expected.

Atti would have his work cut out to select his best team and keep the substitutes happy. He said he'd announce the team on the day of the game because he needed as much time to think about it as possible. It was a shame that some people would probably only play a small part in such a big game, or even miss out altogether. But that was just one outcome of playing high-pressure football.

Conversation in the car was minimal, and Megs began to get nervous as every minute passed. His iPod was tucked firmly into his ears, but he couldn't settle on the songs he wanted, constantly chopping and changing, looking for just the right one.

Before long, the Morrison car was pulling into the car park of the ground. It was the same arena where

Pennendale had beaten Fairfield the week before – a happy place for the Wanderers, and a conspiracy as far as the Sharks were concerned.

The car park was still quite empty, and Megs looked at the clock on the car dashboard. It was an hour and a quarter before kick-off. Atti had asked the team to be there an hour before the game started so he could announce the team, but so far only Megs and Biscan had arrived. Megs recognised Atti's car, but the old man himself was nowhere to be seen.

Before long, players from both teams started to arrive. As the first few Wanderers strolled towards the change-rooms to put their bags inside, Atti's head appeared, saying: 'Out! You little people – OUT! It not time to be in here yet! Five minutes, five minutes!' He shooed the kids away from the door. They were more than confused.

'OUT!'

'Think he might be nervous?' Matteo asked Megs with a grin.

'Never can tell what Atti's gonna do,' Adam laughed.

'But I guess he knows what he's doing,' Megs replied, more hopeful than assured.

Before long all the Vootball Kids had arrived, and they milled about outside the change-rooms, waiting for Atti's call. They were intrigued to see what he had planned, but too nervous to enter without being invited.

By now, there were plenty of red-and-black-tracksuited Sharks players at the ground. They were standing in a group in the distance and looked taller than Megs had remembered. Their parents were madly erecting banners around the section of the grandstand not already taken by the Pennendale fan club.

Fifty-five minutes before kick-off, Atti's head poked around the door to the change-rooms. 'OK, little people. Now is time. Come in, come in. But only players, no parents. And Val too, of course.'

The Pennendale players scooped up their bags (Megs with two hands and a straining back) and made their way inside.

'Wow!'

'Incredible!'

'Good work, Atti!'

'Amazing!'

Inside, Atti had gone to town. There were blue streamers hanging from the ceiling, and pictures of footballers stuck all over the main wall. Football magazines were stacked neatly on the table against the far wall, and above every peg he had stuck the name of a Vootball Kid – including a spot for Val in the far corner. On the bench beneath each peg there was a folder, one for every player. On the main wall among the pictures was a massive white sheet with big blue letters saying: 'Let the ball dance'. As Megs entered the room, he felt a surge of confidence, and he could see it was the same for the others.

They probably couldn't quite put their finger on it, thought Megs, but he knew that each of them felt a little bit different after seeing what Atti had done to the room.

He had made each of them feel more like a player. Maybe only a little bit, but every little boost would count if they were to get over the line.

'OK, sit, sit. No, not there for you, Mr Max! You can't read? Your name is on wall. You sit there!'

'Righto, Atti,' Max replied aimiably.

As they found their spots and sat, each of them began opening the folder that was in their place.

Megs opened his, and began reading:

> Megs,
> You are inspiration of this team. I think you not know it, but you play with energy, skill and commitment, and people follow you playing well. Also, you make this team happen from the start.

Megs looked up. The room was silent, and everyone had their heads in their folders. Only Atti's footsteps could be heard as he limped nervously in circles. Megs continued, his heart beating strongly.

> All you have to do today is enjoy the pressure. And to help you, you are Captain today. You deserve it.

Megs forgot to breathe.

> Remember though, you only try to dribble past someone to get in a better position. If you already in good position, pass or shoot. Play the ball to Paloma on the ground, and don't go too far back when we defending. You are attacking midfielder, not centre defender – you can't do everything.

Let the ball dance, Mr Megs. One day we read about YOU in Shoot magazine, I sure of it.

If Mount Everest had been in front of him, Megs would've skipped up it. And by the look of the other players around him, similar things were written in each of the folders. Not everybody was happy, though, and Megs did see some disappointed faces. Their folders had told them they had not made the starting eleven.

'OK, OK, everyone. You each played big part to getting here, and everything I write in every folder is true. I am sorry I can only pick eleven to start. So here is the team that will start the game.' Atti became very matter-of-fact from that point, and quickly wrote the team on the whiteboard.

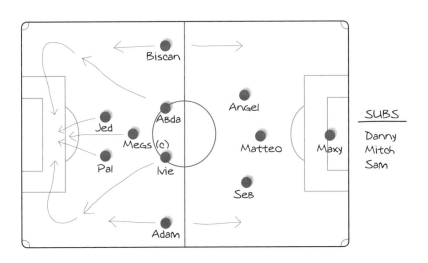

The only surprise was the inclusion of Abda in one of the midfield positions. Atti read the Kids' minds and, looking directly at Abda, said, 'The referee is same as last week. He let you play last week, he will let you play this week. Just like I said in your folder, don't even think about that any more. And that goes for all of you. As far as we concerned, the situation with Abda is old news. You must all be prepared to play knowing she will be part of team.' Paloma, sitting next to Abda, gave her a quick sideways hug. Abda beamed.

The Wanderers were set to play an attacking formation to try and score early on. Atti thought the Sharks would have learnt from the last time the two teams met, when Pennendale had caught the Sharks offside so often. They would probably change their tactics for today, but the Wanderers would be ready.

'And captain for today is Mr Megs.' Megs's face burned with pride as the team clapped Atti's abrupt announcement. 'Right, then, tracksuits on or off I don't care – let's go warm up.'

The Vootball Kids sprang from their seats as if they'd collectively sat on a pin, and burst free from the change-rooms. It was time to make the ball dance.

It was a bitter clash right from the start. But despite all the excitement (or perhaps because of it) the Wanderers started poorly.

They just couldn't do anything right. Passes missed

the target, balls were miscontrolled. The effort was there, but for some reason, they were second to every ball and slow to react. Much as their minds were willing, their bodies didn't seem able to cope.

On the other hand, the Sharks were flying. They seemed faster, bigger and stronger than Pennendale. Somehow older. Even their section of the crowd was winning the vocal battle against the Pennendale supporters.

In the Pennendale goal, Max was keeping the Wanderers in the match. He made save after save, and along with some desperate defending and the lucky intervention of the goalpost (twice), the score remained 0-0 after fifteen minutes.

The spirit of the Wanderers seemed all but squashed, and it was only a matter of time before the Sharks scored. In the end, it came from the left wing. The Sharks' midfield won the ball, then fed it out to their winger. He raced down the line, beat Seb with ease, then cut the ball back into the middle. Their big striker, Thompson, had time to control the ball, turn, and casually pick his spot down low to Max's right and into the back of the net. It was clinical, it was precise... and it was 1–0.

And just before half-time, it became 2–0. A horrible mix-up in the Pennendale defence meant the ball wasn't cleared properly. The Sharks seized on the mistake in a flash and showed no mercy. With beautiful precision, two of them interchanged passes to create some space, then – BANG – the shot was riffled past Max's head with such venom that he didn't even see it until it was in the 'onion bag' (as Megs sometimes called the net).

The Sharks' goal-scorer celebrated wildly, but went too far. He ran the length of the pitch, first past his own supporters, then down in front of the Pennendale fans. There, he made a point of stopping, then walking around as if he was drunk, sticking out his tongue and waving his arms. The referee (and some Sharks team-mates) managed to calm him down, but as he jogged back to the pitch for the restart, he intentionally bumped into Jed, knocking him onto the ground. Jed leapt to his feet in an attempt to get back to the Shark scorer, but Megs and Abda managed to keep him at bay. Things were becoming unpleasant as the Wanderers got frustrated and the Sharks became increasingly smug.

Even in the stands, things were becoming heated. Some of the Sharks' fans were chanting songs intended solely to put the Wanderers off – and it was working.

Not a moment too soon for the Wanderers, it was half-time. In reality it could've been worse than 2–0, and they knew they were in trouble. They walked off silently with their heads bent, as the Sharks jogged off to the break giving high fives and waving to the crowd.

Seventeen | Up to Them

The Vootball Kids made it into the change-rooms and sat despondent. *Atti will set this straight*, Megs thought. The posters and streamers seemed out of place now.

The Kids didn't know it at that point, but Atti wasn't going into the change-rooms. Bizarrely, he stayed outside, choosing to remain alone on the bench.

After a few silent minutes, Megs looked out the window and saw the old school cleaner sitting by himself. The Vootball Kids, he knew, were thoroughly confused as they waited for their coach to come limping in and tell them what was wrong. *Everyone out there must be just as bamboozled*, he thought.

But there was nothing.

The clock ticked.

Just them.

Megs started to chew his nails.

More than two minutes passed. *Where was Atti?* This was THE game to win, and they were throwing it away. They needed their coach to tell them what to do, and they were running out of time! Megs began to get annoyed.

Inside, the Wanderers were growing restless. Jed was pacing the room like a caged tiger. He punched the side of a locker in frustration.

Megs rubbed his face with his hands, then squeezed some sweat out of his hair. As he did so, he saw the captain's armband around his left sleeve. Something clicked inside him, and he spoke.

'You know what? Does anyone here think we're playing well?' No-one answered.

'And is anyone here enjoying themselves?' Silence.

'I don't know what's happened to us today, but I do know that we still have another half to go. Maybe we all got too excited. Maybe... I dunno... maybe we thought we'd won by just getting here. Or maybe we thought we'd done enough by getting Abda to play. I dunno. But we have half a match to put it right.'

Silent voices and fidgety feet.

Megs continued. There was determination in his voice. 'Seriously, if we were playing these punks at lunchtime or in the street, we'd be killing 'em. But we're not. It's as if we've never met each other or something! But Man United did it against Bayern Munich in the Champions League Final a few years ago. They were 2–0 down as well. And what about Liverpool against AC Milan in the 2005 Final – 3–0 down, brought it back to 3–3 before winning on penalties!'

Jed agreed. 'Yeah, let's just do what we do. We can't lose to these idiots!' He was obviously still angry at getting knocked off his feet earlier.

The Kids were lifting up their heads and looking at each other.

Matteo didn't speak much, but when he did, it was usually worth listening. 'Atti can't do anything more. Maybe that's what he's trying to tell us.' He spoke urgently. 'It's up to us, guys!'

There was a knock on the change-room door. It was the ref. 'Let's go, Pennendale. Second half.'

As they purposefully started making their way back to the field, something Mr Mac once said to Megs in England came back to him: *Leadership is not words, it's actions.* Megs was going to have to turn this around, or they were never going to win that trip.

The last thing he saw as he left the change-rooms made him smile. He read: 'Let the ball dance' in big, blue, handwritten letters.

'Come on, the Wanderers!' he called out at the top of his lungs.

Pennendale began the second half sharply, and were moving with a renewed zest. Megs was vocal and encouraging, and the team began showing signs that they were back to the way they'd been all season.

On the other hand, the Sharks started out conservatively, seemingly content to try and play out the game protecting their two-goal advantage. They knew Pennendale needed to score at least three goals to take the championship. Even a draw would be enough for the red-and-blacks to take the title and win the trip.

The very first opportunity for a tackle in the half fell to Jed, and he made sure to win it with gusto. He sprang to his feet after the challenge, took possession of the ball, and immediately knocked it wide to Biscan. This set the tone for the rest of the Pennendale players.

Megs was beavering around the opposition, nipping at their heels and annoying them until he got that ball. Little Anfield would've been proud, he thought. And when in possession, he was very direct. His intensity was back; his legs no longer felt like they were made of lead.

And just on ten minutes, the Wanderers grabbed a goal back. It was Ivie who set it up, after Abda had beaten one player in midfield, then passed a short ball to him. The lanky midfielder had his head up as the ball was coming to him, and already knew where he was going to pass it before it even arrived. Without taking a touch to control it, he whacked it forward into a gap just in front of Paloma. His quick thinking caught the defenders off-guard, and sent Paloma through on goal.

Up to that point, Paloma had hardly had a touch - but she was concentrating for when she did. Her long, dark hair streamed out behind her as she sped forward. Just as she entered the penalty box, she saw a Sharks defender bearing down on her from the left. She shaped to shoot, but just as she was about to pull the trigger, faked, stepped on the ball, and rolled it behind her. Both she and the defender continued to move forward, and the ball sat up perfectly for Jed who had worked hard to be up in support. He ran onto the ball in perfect stride, and with no-one in front of him, kept his head over the ball and struck it low to the keeper's left – 2–1, and what a goal to get back in it!

The Simpfenator didn't even stop to celebrate. He just kept on running, went straight past the keeper on the ground, and picked the ball out of the net. Sticking it under his arm, he ran back to the centre circle, followed by his team-mates. They meant business.

After that, the game got rough. Neither team took a backward step, and the same went for the spectators. Flags were flying and banners were waving. Hardly anyone was sitting any more. No substitutes were made by Pennendale because they were getting on top. The Sharks, however, changed two players to try and inject some new energy to their side.

Loving the competitive cut-and-thrust, Megs started to turn it on. He was everywhere the ball was, winning possession, dribbling past defenders and keeping the Wanderers ticking.

Max was no longer busy in the Pennendale goal, but he kept himself involved by calling instructions to his defenders and encouraging his team-mates. The excitement increased as every second whizzed by. And so the game went until there were eight minutes left.

By now, Megs was running the midfield. Slightly to the left of centre of the ground and therefore in front of the grandstand, he received a firm pass from Seb. His control wasn't perfect, and the ball bobbed up to about thigh height. One of the Sharks players saw that as the moment to charge towards the little Englishman, but Megs was too quick. Before the ball even hit the ground, he'd chipped it up in an arc and moved his body so that the defender went zipping past – directly under the flight of the ball.

'SOMBRERO!'

Megs recognised his Dad's voice from the sidelines, and got a rush of adrenaline. As he dribbled purposefully down the left wing, another defender came towards him. But with a dip of the shoulder and a swivel of his hips, Megs darted past him and continued to attack. He got his head up and saw Abda in support, as well as Adam charging down the wing on an overlapping run.

He had options to pass, but there was only one thing on his mind as the next defender closed him down. It'd been too long. Even at training, things had been getting too serious. Time to set things straight. Time to let the ball dance.

Megs shaped to move the ball on to Adam, who was calling loudly in front of Megs and wider to the left. The defender stretched his leg to block the expected pass… unaware that Megs was never going to pass.

In an instant, the Englishman deftly flicked the ball back in the opposite direction… and straight between the defender's legs.

'NUTMEGS!'

This time it was the Simpfenator's voice he heard. Clapping and laughter rang out in the stands. A few cheeky whistles could also be heard. Megs was loving it.

He took one more touch, then played the ball inside

to Abda. She twisted to control, then gracefully moved forward as a defender came to her. Quickly, she played the ball to the right, just as Paloma made a darting run away from her defender.

Abda kept moving forward, calling out for a return pass. Paloma promptly obliged. The move cut straight through the defence, and set Abda clear in front of goal. Without hesitation, she side-footed the ball to the bottom right corner. As Atti had said about a zillion times during training: 'Ball is small, goal is big. Put ball in corner and keeper stands no chance.' Two–all, and now it really was game on.

This time there were celebrations. Abda jumped high and pumped her fist into the air. Paloma came running to greet her, pumping her own fist up and down and making truck noises. So much for taking Megs's advice about the truck horn celebration!

The blue half of the grandstands were hugging and cheering uncontrollably. Drinks went flying and food ended up on the floor. Atti had every one of the substitutes next to him on the bench in a bear hug. In short, there was pandemonium. And somewhere among the celebrating mass, Abda's dad was crying like a baby.

But two–all wasn't enough, and the Wanderers had to keep pushing. The Sharks were on the back foot, but all they had to do was hold on for another seven minutes. Just like the creatures in the sea that scared Megs half to death, Southside were fierce, strong and proud, and didn't want anybody in their territory. But this was a football field, not the wilds of the ocean, and that ferocity got the team into trouble.

Biscan burst downfield in another Pennendale attack, and cut his way into the penalty area. One of the Sharks' defenders came powering across to cover as the goalkeeper came out to close down the angles. He missed the ball completely, and ended up sawing at Biscan's legs. The crowd were appalled and let their feelings be known. Biscan lay writhing on the ground.

'Come on, ref! Sort it out!' Jed called to the ref as he ran to see if Biscan was OK.

But the ref had already sorted it out. With a sense of theatre, he called the defender to him. Standing almost eye-to-eye with the Shark, the referee reached for something in his top pocket. With finger and thumb, he purposefully pulled out a card. It was yellow and shiny and stood out against the crystal blue sky.

But quickly he waved his left hand and shook his head, as his right hand reached in again. This time, the card was red. He'd made a mistake the first time... the shark was off!

A section of the Pennendale crowd couldn't resist, and started to chant 'Off... off... off... off!' as the dejected player made his way slowly from the pitch. The Sharks' supporters went crazy with disgust.

But there was more drama to follow.

Biscan had a massive smile on his face as he limped to his feet with the aid of his team-mates. The referee was, quite rightly, pointing to the penalty spot.

So, two–all with three minutes to go. This was the golden opportunity for the Wanderers to score what would doubtless be the final goal of the game. The title was surely just one kick away.

Megs wanted to score the goal that won them the Championship. Some players shy away from that sort of pressure, but Megs was happy to take responsibility. And he was captain, after all.

The players gradually cleared the area as Megs carefully placed the ball on the spot. He noticed the ball was starting to lose some of its shine, and that two of the stitches were coming apart. On the sidelines, Mr and Mrs Morrison stood linked together in complete silence. Mrs Morrison's Bulldogs beanie was clasped firmly in her left hand. Even Anfield seemed to sense the tension and stood still for probably the first time in her life!

Megs made sure the ball was well placed, then he stood upright, turned and walked back to take the kick. He didn't look at the 'keeper.

The arena was silent.

The referee blew his whistle.

Megs now looked up at the goalkeeper, crouched on his line and ready to pounce.

Megs waited. And so did the keeper.

Some expectant noise started up in the crowd – as well as from some of the Sharks players hoping to put Megs off.

Still he waited.

Then the goalkeeper stood upright to ask about the delay – just the thing Megs was waiting for. Immediately, he began his run-up to the ball. Quickly, the keeper got himself ready again.

Megs wanted the bottom left-hand corner, and was reminding himself not to kick the ball too hard. Just place it.

The ball was struck cleanly, and headed for that bottom corner. The keeper dived too soon, in the wrong direction, and...

THUD!

The ball cannoned into the post, then bounced clear of the goals. Megs dropped to his knees.

He'd missed.

The Sharks players were delirious. They hugged and jumped and screamed with joy. Their supporters did the same.

Megs felt his stomach drop to his toes. He wanted the earth to swallow him whole. He'd cost Pennendale the title, and lost his team the trip to England.

'Come on, Sharks, I've stopped the clock – take the goal kick.' The referee was struggling to get the game going again among the chaos. Only two minutes plus injury time remained.

Paloma grabbed Megs's arms and silently dragged him to his feet. As they moved back into position to await the goal kick, Megs looked towards the bench. Expecting to see a dejected coach slumped in the corner, he was surprised to see that Atti was standing, smiling his crooked smile. Then he shrugged his shoulders as if to say, 'Oh well' and called out, 'You still have two minutes, Mr Megs. You can't give up yet!'

Atti was right. Gerrard wouldn't give up. Little Anfield would never give up. Megs wasn't going to give up either.

The goal kick went long, and dropped around the centre of the pitch. There was a scramble in the middle, before Southside booted the ball long into Pennendale's half of the pitch. Matteo read it well and comfortably took control. Calmly, he lifted his eyes and scanned the pitch in front of him. He took a touch forward, then assessed the situation again. Megs saw an opportunity and made a darting run across to the right wing. Matteo spotted him and knocked a beautifully weighted pass straight over to the little Englishman.

Sections of the crowd were whistling to try and persuade the referee to end the game. But that was the furthest thing from Megs's mind, as he sprinted down the wing. A Sharks defender sped towards him, but without the desperation that was driving the Pennendale star. Megs zipped past the defender as if he wasn't there, and powered on.

Meanwhile, as many Pennendale players as possible swarmed forward to support Megs and get onto the attack.

Megs shimmied and twisted past another defender, then turned inside. Another Shark came at him, so he flicked the ball behind his leg, and angled his run back out to the wing.

The same player that Megs had nutmegged earlier made his way over to defend once again. Obviously concerned that Megs might embarrass him again, he didn't stretch his leg to try and block Megs's cross.

But Megs had seen a darting run, and knew he had

to get the ball into the Sharks' penalty box as quickly as possible. From the corner of his eye, Megs now saw it was Paloma bolting across the box towards the near post.

Replicating some of their kickabouts in the Morrison garden (but with roles reversed) Megs clipped a swerving cross beyond the defender and superbly into Paloma's onrushing path. In the garden, Megs had always aimed for a spectacular diving header, but headers and Paloma were like Vegemite on top of ice-cream – they just didn't mix.

As the ball spun through the air, Paloma didn't stop to think. On the edge of the six-yard box, she launched her body towards the advancing ball. Her neck edged back as she twisted her body mid-air to allow an angle towards goal. Her eyes were mere slits (yes, she was still scared), but this was the chance to win the match.

BANG!

The ball cannoned off her forehead with tremendous force, and flew towards the Sharks' goal. The keeper could only watch as the ball powered into the roof of the net.

GOAL!!!

All hell broke loose. Paloma had no time even to get off the ground before her team-mates hurled themselves onto her. Atti pumped his fists with joy on the sidelines, and gazed up to the heavens. Mr and Mrs Morrison bounced on the spot with Paloma's parents in what looked like a four-way Wrestle Mania competition on a trampoline. The Sharks players (and their parents) sank to their knees in despair.

It was the last piece of action in the match, and a thrilling way to end the season. Repeated chants of 'We're going to En-ger-land' rang out across the pitch.

Megs found Atti amid the chaos. The old man threw two spindly arms around the young star, his eyes glazed over with the beginning of tears. His brain had obviously got stuck on two words that he said over and over to any Vootball Kid within earshot: 'Thank you, thank you. Thank you!'

'No, thank *you*,' was all Megs could manage from underneath his ecstatic coach's armpit, but Atti was too happy to hear him. When Megs managed to wriggle free, he saw Paloma, and the two connected the loudest, stingyest high five imaginable. 'Well done, Raul – your first header!' Megs teased.

'Yeah, and hopefully my last,' she replied happily, rubbing her forehead.

Megs then got wrapped up in strong, familiar pairs of arms. It was his parents, beaming with delight. 'Brilliant, son. You sure turned it on today!' said his dad.

Mrs Morrison planted an embarrassingly long kiss on his cheek and hugged Megs's sweaty body to within an inch of its life. 'Mu-ummm!' he wailed.

Meanwhile, little Anfield was leaping about, pawing at Megs's leg, wanting in on the action. Her stumpy little tail was wagging so fast it looked as though she might take off at any moment.

As his mum released Megs for a split second, Matteo, Adam, Biscan and Jed all came piling in to tackle him to the ground and stack on top of him, ruffling his hair and singing, 'Champions, champions, champions!' over and over. Soon, Max, Seb and Danny joined the heap – with little Anfield doing her best to climb on as well.

Meanwhile, the girls were crowding around each other, bouncing as they hugged. Abda's headscarf bobbed up and down, her face transformed with joy. Val had lost her notebook in the bedlam.

Even some of the parents were overcome, thoroughly embarrassing their kids by wiping away tears. Mrs Mendez was the worst, hugging any kid who stood still long enough to be captured, tears flowing down her cheeks.

The joyous scene of those in blue was in stark contrast to the red-and-black picture. The Sharks players were sitting on the ground in silence, while their parents paced angrily, finding reasons for their team's slump. Megs tried to feel sorry for them but kept remembering their attempt to undermine the Wanderers' chances quickly. His pity dried up.

The celebrations continued mid-pitch, and the camera operators snapped madly away as Mr Morrison and Mr Mendez lifted Atti onto their shoulders. Unlike before, even Abda was happy to pose for photos with her team-mates and family.

'Megs, Megs, come here for a second!' It was Mrs Morrison again, calling her son over to the edge of the crowd. Mr Morrison and Anfield were by her side. All of them, even Anfield, seemed to be beaming.

'What a day, huh! Well done.' Megs's mum looked at

him proudly. 'Now listen, we want to ask you something. Do you mind if we all come to England for this trip? Would that be OK?'

Megs looked across at his dad, who had a sly grin plastered across his face.

Megs's stomach was doing cartwheels. 'Does this mean – ?'

'Yep!' said Mr Morrison. 'We're staying in Australia. I got a major client in Thailand and two small ones in Vietnam. And Vincent signed up a big one here as well. So the company is back on track. Didn't want to tell you this morning before the game.'

'And to celebrate,' finished Mrs Morrison, 'we thought we'd like to share the trip back home –'

'Except that... home is here now,' Megs corrected softly, believing it for the first time.

He threw his arms around his dad's waist, and then his mum joined in the team hug. Only Anfield didn't know why everyone was so excited, but she participated with a few cheerful yaps of her own anyway.

The End...

ROUND 18 - FINAL TABLE				
CLUB	W	L	D	Pts
Pennendale Wanderers	**13**	**2**	**3**	**42**
Southside Sharks	13	3	2	41
Hills Rockets	9	4	5	32
Penders Grove	9	4	5	32
Brenthill Catholic	9	5	4	31
Roverdale	5	4	9	24
Fairfield	5	6	7	22
Thornbury	3	10	6	15
Trengal Tigers	2	11	5	11
Bayside Blues	0	15	3	3

About the Authors

Mark

It is nearly a decade now since Mark Schwarzer established himself as not only Australia's premium goalkeeper, but one of the world's best. With his quick reactions and innate composure, Mark has taken his career from humble beginnings in rural New South Wales to become a mainstay of what most sportspeople consider the greatest football league in the world, the English Premier League.

After spending his school days at North Richmond Primary and Colo High School, Mark made his impact on the Australian League (then the NSL) at the age of nineteen, and quickly entrenched himself as a regular by guiding his side, Marconi Fairfield, to the NSL championship. Mark's talent was quickly recognised by overseas scouts and at the age of twenty-one he was signed by Dynamo Dresden in Germany. After temporary stops at clubs Kaiserslautern and Bradford City, Mark found his home at Middlesbrough where the wiry Australian is now the longest-serving player and has notched up over 300 matches.

Mark's heroics in the penalty shootout that got Australia to the 2006 World Cup will forever be remembered as a highlight in Australian sport, but they were just a small part of his ongoing Socceroo story that began with penalty saves against Canada in 1993.

Mark is just under two metres tall (6 foot 5 inches), has worn the same pair of shin pads since turning professional as a nineteen-year-old in 1992, and speaks three languages (English, German and Spanish). He lives in the north of England and is married to Paloma. They have two children, Julian and Amaya. After living in Europe since 1994, he looks forward to the day when the family will come home to Sydney's sunny shores.

Neil

Neil Montagnana-Wallace was born in Australia, but his father is Scottish, his mother is English and his brother is American. His wife is Italian-Australian, and when they got married, they decided to stick their names together and make the most confusing surname in the world.

Neil was a handy soccer player who didn't make it in England, but has played in Victoria's State Leagues for fifteen years. He's a Senior Licence coach, and wrote Our Socceroos in 2004 (www. oursocceroos.com) - which was how he struck up a friendship with Mark and ultimately how the seeds of Megs were sown. Earlier, he was Marketing and Events Manager at the Football Federation of Victoria.

The young Neil grew up in Castle Hill, NSW where he attended Castle Hill Primary and James Ruse before moving to Melbourne and going to Melbourne High School. After living in Rome in 2005, Neil now speaks Italian, and has learnt to enjoy olives. He lives in Melbourne with his wife Val, young son, Finn and a cat called Flash. When not writing, Neil is the Marketing and Strategy Director of Woof Creative Solutions.

In England Neil supports Coventry City; in Italy he supports Roma; in Scotland he supports Dunfermline and in Australia he supports Melbourne Victory. His record for juggling is 891, and his career highlight was one glorious training session years ago where he managed six beautiful nutmegs.

Don't forget to check out...

Megs & The Vootball Kids

Truth was, he didn't know anything about Australia except that it was a long way away, it was sunny, there were kangaroos, his friends weren't there, and they called football 'soccer'. What was there to look forward to about that?

Edward 'Megs' Morrison is starting at a new school. That's hard enough, but to do it in a foreign land makes it even more uncomfortable. At least Megs speaks the language… sort of.

Luckily, football is an international password, and football just happens to be something Edward Morrison loves – but his new school doesn't have a proper team, because no one is available to coach.

Megs makes an unlikely friend of a quirky old Hungarian school cleaner, but will he ever make friends his own age? Will he ever feel at home on the other side of the planet? And with no school team, how will Megs quench his thirst for competitive football?

Megs and The Vootball Kids is a story about persistence, dedication and overcoming obstacles. It's about making a difference whatever your background… and it's about football.

Coming Soon...

Megs & The Crazy Legs

The pitch was marked out with two hundred numbered squares. Gone were the 18 yard box, the centre circle and the penalty spot. The cow wandered around aimlessly, oblivious to the fact that what must have been nearly two hundred and fifty people were watching. And waiting.

Football opens doors to a sometimes strange, always interesting world, and the Wanderers' continuing story is no different. Book Three in the Megs series deals with new faces, new crazy-legged tricks and an entirely new world.

There's jealousy, laughs, hardship and gossip... and there's an international brand of football to deal with.

For exclusive extracts and notification of the book's release, join the Wanderers' Fan Club. You might even win an advanced copy signed by the authors!

COMING SOON TO megsmorrison.com

Also by the Authors...

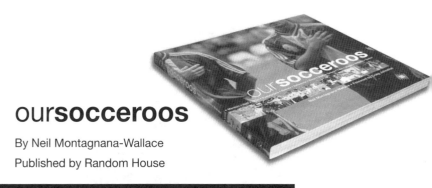

our**socceroos**

By Neil Montagnana-Wallace
Published by Random House

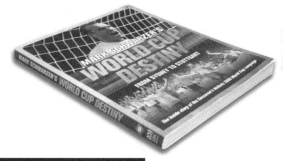

WORLD CUP DESTINY

By Mark Schwarzer
Published by ABC Books

JOIN THE CLUB!

Megs and the Vootball Kids would love you to join the Wanderers' Fan Club. All you have to do is go to www.megsmorrison.com, and follow the 'join the club' link. It's FREE, and you'll get;

A certificate from Mark, Neil and Megs

Exclusive extracts from upcoming books

The chance to email Mark and Neil (and Megs!)

Exclusive news and information from Mark and Neil

The chance to get advance copies of future books

The chance to win great prizes, like;

Signed Mark Schwarzer Socceroo tops
Signed Mark Schwarzer gloves
A chance to interview Mark Schwarzer
Copies of Megs signed by the authors
A trip by the authors to your school

… and much more to be announced. Stay tuned!

Launching *Megs & The Vootball Kids*